BREWED, CRUDE AND TATTOOED

The new 'Maggy Thorsen' coffee-house mystery

When Maggy Thorsen, co-owner of coffee-house Uncommon Grounds, is trapped in a shopping mall by a snow storm, which cuts the electricity and phone lines, she finds the body of Way Benson, the owner of the mall. Maggy's discovery unearths other refugees of the storm and more than one of these people has a motive for killing the arrogant Way. Then there is another murder...

Sandra Balzo titles available from
Severn House Large Print

Bean There, Done that
Grounds for Murder

BREWED, CRUDE AND TATTOOED

A Maggy Thorsen Mystery

Sandra Balzo

Severn House Large Print
London & New York

This first large print edition published 2010
in Great Britain and the USA by
SEVERN HOUSE PUBLISHERS LTD of
9-15 High Street, Sutton, Surrey, SM1 1DF.
First world regular print edition published 2009 by
Severn House Publishers Ltd., London and New York.

British Library Cataloguing in Publication Data

Balzo, Sandra.
  Brewed, crude and tattooed.
  1. Thorsen, Maggy (Fictitious character)--Fiction.
  2. Coffeehouses--Wisconsin--Milwaukee--Fiction.
  3. Businesswomen--Wisconsin--Milwaukee--Fiction.
  4. Detective and mystery stories. 5. Large type books.
  I. Title
  813.6-dc22

  ISBN-13: 978-0-7278-7857-1

Severn House Publishers support The Forest Stewardship
Council [FSC], the leading international forest certification
organisation. All our titles that are printed on Greenpeace-
approved FSC-certified paper carry the FSC logo.

Printed and bound in Great Britain by the
MPG Books Group, Bodmin, Cornwall.

ONE

The morning of the 'Perfect Spring Storm', as it was later dubbed, dawned dark and warm.

Of course, that depends on your definition of dawn. Or even warm, for that matter.

To me, Maggy Thorsen, 'dawn' means whenever I have to wake up to stumble out of the house, usually into the dark, to open my coffeehouse, Uncommon Grounds, in Benson Plaza.

That May day, my dawn was at five a.m., the sun not even a faint glow on the horizon. And while 'warm' was technically a matter of degrees – Fahrenheit, in Wisconsin – I measured it more in degrees of undress.

Sticking my nose out the door as my sheepdog Frank watered the hyacinths, I decided it was a T-shirt and jeans day. Which, just west of Milwaukee, qualifies as warm.

'C'mon, Frank, hurry up,' I said in a stage whisper, so as not to disturb my neighbors. I

5

liked to think the whisper was quieter than my normal speaking voice – probably deluding myself, like the 'shushers' in theaters, who make more noise than the people they're shushing.

'Shush!' came from the direction of my neighbor's bedroom and then the window slammed down. Three dogs started to bark at the sound and Frank joined in.

'Shush, Frank,' I said in another stage whisper.

I herded my sheepdog up the porch steps, neither of us commenting on the irony.

I was hurrying this beautiful morning because I'd decided to walk to Uncommon Grounds, less than a mile away. The early hours have always been stolen treasures for me. Time that I wasn't taking away from my son Eric, before he went to college, or my husband Ted, before we divorced.

Walking through the dark, but toward the sunrise, can be a rare pleasure.

Besides, my car was in the shop.

Frank lugged into the living room ahead of me and turned. Had I been able to see under all the hair, I knew there would be accusation in his eyes.

'I know, I short-changed piddle time,' I said, apologetically. 'Tell you what: I'll come back on my lunch hour.'

The record for Frank's longest urinary stream was ninety-three seconds. I didn't have that margin this morning. 'We'll go for a walk then,' I offered feebly.

Through his sheepdog bangs, Frank just looked at me. I think.

'I won't forget,' I said, picking up my handbag. 'I swear.'

Frank turned his back on me and padded to the hearth. He circled, managing to sling sheepdog drool a full 360 degrees before settling on the floor with a 'hummph'.

Cowed, I flipped on the television set. 'Look, Frank,' I said. 'The WTVR Morning Show. You can watch all the pretty girls.'

Frank lifted his head and then, apparently remembering his pique, turned up his nose at both me and the TV.

Ah well, he'd get over it. Maybe I'd bring us both home a ham sandwich. Buoyed by the thought, I let myself out the door.

I was barely a block away when I realized that the temperature wasn't quite as warm as I'd imagined, and I hadn't brought even a light coat. In fact, it seemed to be colder now than it was when I'd let Frank out just minutes before.

A smart woman would have turned around

and gotten at least a jacket.

I am not that woman. In fact, I'm the kind of woman who can be intimidated by her own sheepdog. Though it could be worse. Frank could be a hamster.

Rather than facing my pet again, I kept going, figuring that the sun would rise soon and the warm-up could begin. I was wrong, though a jacket or even a coat at that point wouldn't have changed any of the events of the coming day.

My post-divorce house – blue stucco walls, puke-green toilets, and all – is north of Uncommon Grounds on Poplar Creek Drive. Poplar Creek Drive, as you might expect, parallels Poplar Creek, which runs north to south. The farther downstream you go, the nicer (read: more expensive) the houses. I am as far *up*stream as you can get and still remain in Brookhills, unless I wanted to take up residence at Christ Christian Church, just north of me. I didn't, and I feared that was more than fine with them.

As I crossed Poplar Creek Drive, two kids on bicycles came roaring out of the dark in front of me.

'Hey, watch it!'

The teens were already well past and probably didn't even hear me. The neighborhood dogs did, though, and sent up a racket.

Maggy Thorsen, bringing joy to everyone, everywhere, at five thirty a.m.

'Shut up!' came from one of the houses.

'Shush, Chivas.' Another, next door.

'Come in here now, Skylar.' A smooth, aristocratic voice.

Maybe because I usually drive to work, I had never noticed how many people were up at this time of the morning. Kids on bikes. Cars in driveways, doors wide open. Police officers...

Uh-oh.

A Brookhills police cruiser was parked at the curb, roof lights flashing as they revolved. Standing in the driveway next to a Hyundai was Sophie Daystrom, one of Uncommon Grounds' most faithful customers. Despite being an octogenarian with a fixed income, Sophie had managed to hang on to her house – no easy task, given Brookhills' rising property taxes.

Sophie'd once told me that her monthly taxes were three times what the mortgage total had been when she and her late husband bought the house.

'Is everything OK?' I asked now, walking up the driveway.

Besides drinking coffee at Uncommon

Grounds, Sophie found time to volunteer at the religious bookstore next to us in Benson Plaza, and was the newly elected queen of the local Red Hat Society – a group of women devoted to friendship and staying active.

However, none of the above required her to be up at this ungodly hour.

'OK?' Sophie asked. 'Do I look OK? Would I be out here in my frickin' duster at this time of the morning if everything was "OK"?'

Sophie made Frank look cheery. 'In that case, are *you* all right?' I amended.

'Somebody broke into my gosh-darn car.' This from the potty-mouth of The Bible Store. 'The little turds broke into cars all over the neighborhood. They stole my office keys and my tape player. How the heck am I going to listen to my relaxation tapes?'

I wasn't sure, in the interest of public safety, that Sophie should be listening to relaxation tapes while driving, but I tried to sympathize.

'Were the "little turds" in question by any chance riding bicycles?' I asked.

The uniformed police officer, who had been leaning into the Hyundai, stood back up. 'That's what other people have reported.

10

Why? Did you see them?'

I nodded. 'Two kids on bikes sped past me about a block back. They were maybe sixteen or seventeen.' Which was unusual because, at the age of sixteen in Brookhills, a kid's Trek is transformed into a Lexus, as if by magic. Though more typically by Mom and Dad.

On the other hand, a bicycle might make for a quicker and cleaner getaway than a luxury car. Especially if the bike didn't come equipped with GPS.

I gave my information to the officer and hurried on to work, though not quickly enough for my partner Caron Egan, who didn't seem to think crime-busting was much of an excuse for arriving late.

Five hours later, I was still in the dog house, pulling garbage duty.

'Dry scalp?' Sarah Kingston asked, swiping at my hair when I came in from the dumpster corral.

Sarah is a good friend and an even better real-estate agent. She's also about as un-Brookhillsian as a woman can get, though a few months prior Sarah did have a short brush with tennis togs and ladies who do lunch.

Thank God, she'd recovered.

Today Sarah was sporting her usual attire of sensible shoes, pleated-front trousers and baggy jackets. The only thing missing these days was the pack of Virginia Slims Menthol she used to carry in her right jacket pocket. The lighter had been in the left, apparently so she wouldn't die from spontaneous combustion.

'Very funny.' I shook my hair to dislodge the melting flakes. 'It's snowing like crazy out there.'

And make no mistake: I found nothing particularly humorous about icy crystals parachuting from the sky on May 1st. I didn't give a shit that we were in Wisconsin. Seems to me that even the tundra deserves a spring.

'Will you please freeze?' Caron said, trailing me with a paper towel. 'You're tracking in snow.'

Caron enjoys playing Felix to my Oscar. *The Odd Couple.* Jack Lemmon and Walter Matthau. Rent it on DVD.

I was freezing, all right, but not in the way Caron meant. 'Didn't you hear me?' I asked as she stooped to mop up the slush my canvas sneakers had left behind. 'It's snowing. In May. A lot.'

'I know,' she said. 'Listen, I think I saw a shovel sticking out of a drift when I looked in back.' A sidelong glance. 'Maybe you could clear the front walk?'

I shuddered. I hated shoveling. When we were married, Ted, my ex-husband, and I had a snow plow company clear the snow in our driveway. Now that I was on my own, I couldn't afford to hire anyone except Petey, a misfit neighbor kid who always managed to show up minutes after I'd given up on him and shoveled myself.

Did I mention I hated shoveling? And Petey?

Happily, I had an excuse for dodging the experience this time. 'I'm sorry, Caron, but I don't have a coat here.'

'You can borrow mine,' Sarah offered.

I threw her a dirty look. 'Besides, I'm sure they'll plow the lot and snow-blow the sidewalks soon. That's why we pay a monthly maintenance fee.'

Caron rolled her eyes and stuffed the paper towel in my hand. 'Fine. But then I need to get out the winter floor mats.' She disappeared in the direction of the storeroom.

Sarah raised her eyebrows at me, even as she searched in her pocket for a phantom cigarette.

'They're so people won't track in snow,' I explained. 'Caron doesn't like puddles.'

'Evidently not.' Sarah gave up on the cigarettes and nodded at the pond forming at my feet. 'You're still dripping.'

I dropped the wad of paper towels on the ground and slooshed it back and forth with my toe. 'The TVR Weather Slut lied.'

Caron came back from the storeroom dragging a rolled-up rubber mat. 'Shh,' she said, backing past us. 'The Weather Slut ... I mean, Aurora is Way's ex-wife, and they're still tight. The last thing we need to do is draw attention to ourselves.'

Way Benson was town chairman and owner of Benson Plaza, the strip mall where Uncommon Grounds rented space. That made the toad our landlord, at least for now. Our lease came up for renewal in November and, as other tenants' leases expired, Way hadn't opted to 're-up' them. He had plans for Benson Plaza and none of the current tenants – including, I feared, our little coffee emporium – apparently fit in.

The Plaza is shaped like the letter L, turned on its head. Uncommon Grounds was on the far end of the short side, which faces Brookhill Road, the main drag for suburban commuters heading into downtown Milwaukee. Next to UG on the same side was an old dental office that only the prior week had been converted to The Bible Store, where Sophie worked. At the corner was Rudy's Barbershop.

Continuing down the long side of the L, you had An's Foods, Goddard's Pharmacy and, at the very end of Benson Plaza, Way's management office.

The first store to get an eviction notice was An's Foods. Then, even as owner Tien Romano and her father Luccio – or Luc – emptied their shelves and sold off their deli cases and meat counter equipment, Gloria Goddard at the pharmacy next door got her walking papers. I hadn't heard anything about The Bible Store, which Sophie said was on a month-to-month lease, but word had it that Rudy's Barbershop was also folding its smocks and preparing to silently steal away.

The front door swung open hard, crashing the sleigh bells hanging on it against the plate-glass window. Jacque Oui, fishmonger extraordinaire at Schultz's Market down the street, made a dramatic entrance.

'I am stuck in the ditch. You must call me the Triple A!' he demanded. The veneer of French accent on Jacque's English always grew thicker whenever he was excited or upset.

I looked out our front window. Sure enough, Jacque's ancient little Peugeot was caught as a dying still-life, nose-first in the shallow ditch that separates our parking lot from Brookhill Road.

Sarah joined me at the window. 'Slid off the pavement, huh?'

'Were you going too fast for the conditions?' Caron asked, prodding him with the rolled-up rug, so she could put it down. 'You know when you start to skid you're supposed to take your foot off the gas pedal and—'

'I am not speeding,' Jacque said. 'Your ditch, it is too close to the road.'

I ignored that and picked up the phone. As I did, there was a loud boom. I hastily replaced the receiver. 'Holy shit,' I said. 'Was that thunder?'

'I didn't see any lightning,' Sarah said, getting close to the window and craning her neck. 'Did you?'

'Maybe it was an explosion of some kind,' Caron contributed calmly as she rolled out the rug.

The minute she got it down flat, I pulled open the door and stuck my head out. The snow was coming down not so much in flakes but in fistfuls. As I watched, there was a prolonged flash, like a strobe light seen through ground fog at the airport. It was followed by another muffled boom.

'Thundersnow,' I said delightedly. 'God, but I love this stuff.'

Sarah shouldered me aside and looked out disgustedly. 'At this rate, it's going to take me half an hour to trudge back to my office. And what happened to the woman who *hates* snow?'

'Thundersnow?' Jacque said, temporarily forgetting his rapidly disappearing car. 'Snow, it does not make the thunder–' another flash – 'or the lightning.'

'Here it does,' I told him authoritatively. My now college-age son Eric had done a report on the phenomenon of thundersnow when he was in the fifth grade. 'But even where we are in the Great Lakes area, it's rare. Seven-hundredths of one percent of snowstorms are thundersnows, somebody estimated.'

I couldn't remember who, of course. Not that it mattered, as Jacque was no longer listening to me. 'The phone?' he said, pointedly.

'Help yourself.' I was still looking out the door.

'It's snowing in,' Caron said to me testily as Sarah shrugged into her coat. 'Will you *please* close that?'

'Let me out first,' Sarah said. 'I always leave my office window open this time of year. I'd better go close it or there'll be drifts on my desk.'

Sarah's real-estate operation was about a block and a half away in what had been a private house. It was charming, far more so than Sarah's manners as she shoved me aside to leave us. From a coat pocket, she drew out a plastic rain bonnet, the kind my mother had worn on her head to protect her 'permanent wave'.

'That's not going to keep you very warm,' I warned. 'Do you want a towel to put over your head?'

'We don't have any towels,' Caron said. 'You took all of ours home to wash and never brought any back.'

Had me there. Not that it mattered. Sarah had waved and was already almost down the length of our leg of the retail mall, just now reaching Rudy's Barbershop.

'I'll be fine,' she yelled and then disappeared into the snow.

'She is dead,' Jacque said from behind me.

TWO

'You think the storm is that bad?' I asked, as a roar built outside. 'Maybe I shouldn't have let Sarah leave.'

He held up the receiver. 'No, no. I speak of your telephone. She is dead.'

Jacque set the phone down and came up behind me to look for the source of the noise. 'That, it is a ... what, motor scooter?'

Tough to see through the white-out, but a two-wheeled vehicle did seem to be cornering into the snow-covered parking lot. As it got closer, I saw that it was a Harley. And Jake Pavlik, who was straddling said motorcycle, would dearly hate to hear his Harley Fat Boy described as a 'scooter'.

Pavlik – he of the dark curly hair and gray/blue eyes – was the Brookhills County Sheriff and my boyfriend. Or main squeeze. Or man-pal.

Whatever.

I was too old to keep up with current

19

terminology for older couples who aren't engaged or married. The 'altared' states at least have titles. Fiancé. Fiancée. Bride. Groom. Even when undone, you were still left with an ex-fiancé(e) or just an ex.

Linguistics aside, though, one of the reasons I was confused about the nature of my relationship with Pavlik was that we'd consummated it only once. OK, twice if you count 'sessions' in one night. Now, I suppose that if you tallied orgasms ... well, none of your business.

Point is, we see a whole lot more of each other in our clothes than out of them. As Pavlik came to the door of Uncommon Grounds, though, I had to admit he looked awfully good even un-naked. Especially in the lean, dark-wash jeans and the soft leather jacket that had become a favorite of mine.

In fact, though I realized it was embarrassingly shallow of me, if Pavlik disappeared, the coat and I might well be very happy together.

Pavlik kissed me on the lips, and I ran my hand over the buttery leather of the jacket. Perfection.

'Everybody OK in here?' Pavlik asked, taking in the huddled masses. 'I saw a car buried in the ditch.'

'Jacque's.' I gestured at the man behind me. 'Officer Caron thinks he was going a bit too fast for the conditions. Speaking of which, should you really be doing a latter-day *Easy Rider* in this weather?'

Pavlik shook his head. 'Nope. I'm heading back to my place to drop off the bike and get a four-wheel drive.' A sheepish smile that warmed my heart, if not the weather. 'I just didn't expect snow at this time of year.'

'Thundersnow,' I said as more of Mother Nature's artillery rumbled. 'Isn't it cool?'

'Isn't it cool?' a voice behind me mimicked disgustedly. Jacque put his palm on my shoulder and nudged me out of the way.

Oui'd better watch himself or I'd tell our new sheriff what Frenchy had called Pavlik's prized hog.

'Sheriff, you give me the hand with my baby?'

Pavlik blinked. 'Your...?'

'My treasure.' Jacque gestured toward his rapidly disappearing car. 'It is the Peugeot, one of many classics from the country of my birth.' He put his hand to his heart. 'I love it the way in which you love your motor scooter.'

'My motor...?'

'Fat Boy,' I furnished.

Pavlik sent me a dark look. Talk about shooting the messenger.

'Please?' Jacque steepled his hands. 'I implore you.'

Pavlik stepped out to get a better look. 'I think we're going to need a third person to get "your baby" out of that ditch.'

The words 'your baby' had a gratifyingly sarcastic edge to them.

'One of us will have to steer,' the sheriff continued, 'while two of us push.'

Brookhills' finest and the French Foreign Legionnaire looked toward me.

'No way, boys. I don't even have a jacket, much less a winter coat.' Which prompted me to eye Pavlik's leather number. 'Unless, of course—'

'Need help?' a voice interrupted. Rudy Fischer, The Barber of Brookhills, had come up behind Pavlik while I was committing faux-foreplay with the sheriff's jacket.

'That'd be great,' Pavlik said, watching me suspiciously as I rubbed the cuff of his sleeve. 'Maybe you can drive while Jacque and I push.'

'I am the only one who will drive the Peugeot,' announced Jacque Oui. 'As I say before, she is my baby.'

Yeah, yeah, yeah – your baby. We get it.

Pavlik hesitated. Although Rudy seemed well-conditioned, he had to be nearing seventy, which transformed 'well-condition-ed' into a relative compliment.

'Not to worry, Sheriff,' Rudy said, sensing Pavlik's indecision. 'My personal trainer says that I'm in better shape than most forty-year-olds.' He looked disparagingly at Jacque, who was probably teetering on the brink of leaving his thirties.

'*My* "personal" trainer?' This time Jacque was mimicking Rudy, which was much more to my liking. 'But, tell me, in what manner does my ex-wife train you?'

Pavlik looked at me, puzzled, but I didn't have any light to shed on what Jacque was talking about.

If Rudy himself understood, he chose to laugh it off. '"To everything there is a sea-son",' he quoted, plucking at the gloves in his pocket. 'And yours, my French prede-cessor, is over.'

I cleared my throat. 'Umm, Jacque. Should we get "your baby" out of the ditch?'

The overly proud papa just nodded stiffly and the three men went out into the storm, wading through the snow like it was water.

Or maybe more like mud.

'The snow is really wet,' I said, turning to

23

Caron.

She was mopping up the drift I'd let in by holding the door open and gave me a dirty, 'tell-me-about-it' look. I turned back and watched as Jacque climbed into the car and started it.

Because the Peugeot was hood-and-bumper into the ditch, Rudy and Pavlik moved in front and pushed, while Jacque put the car into reverse and stepped on the gas. Two or three rocking tries, but no luck. However, on (by my count) the sixth, the Peugeot was finally back on the road.

As Rudy and Pavlik waved, Jacque drove a half-block down Brookhill Road, turned left on to Civic Drive and then left again into the Benson Plaza parking lot, coming to a stop in a space not twenty feet from where his car had been stuck.

I could see Pavlik and Rudy exchange exasperated looks.

'Aren't you going back to Schultz's?' I said to the fishmonger extraordinaire as he came to the door of Uncommon Grounds.

'A cappuccino first, I think,' Jacque said, tracking snow-to-slush over Caron's rug and up to the counter.

With my partner chasing Jacque with more paper towels, it fell to me to make his drink.

A cappuccino is one-third espresso, one-third steamed milk and one-third frothed milk. For myself, I preferred lattes, which are one-third espresso and two-thirds steamed milk, with just a dollop of froth, if any.

Since a latte costs the same as a cappuccino, but contains the same amount of espresso and twice the milk, I figure it's a better deal. Still, if people were willing to pay me for air, in the form of the steam that froths the milk, I was all for it.

'That'll be $4.95,' I said, putting the drink on the counter.

Jacque pulled out his money as Rudy and Pavlik came in. 'I buy you the drink for your help, gentlemen?'

'A cup of black coffee sounds good,' Rudy said, taking off his coat and laying it on the back of a chair.

'Not for me,' Pavlik said. He came around to the open side of the U-shaped front counter and I went to meet him.

He gave me a kiss and I brushed snowflakes off the shoulder of his jacket. Slowly. 'Are you sure you're going to be OK on that bike?'

'Nah, it's gotten too bad out for me to try for home. I just called in to the department, and a squad is going to pick me up.'

'Good,' I said gratefully.

He canted his head toward our picture window. 'All right if I pull the Harley up on to the sidewalk next to your store?'

'Of course.' At least that way any overhang of the roof would protect his bike a bit. 'Why don't you have your deputy drop you back here at six when I get off? The streets should be cleared by then. We can go to my house and I'll make you dinner.'

'Deal,' Pavlik said. 'And maybe we can light a blaze in that big old fireplace of yours.'

And shut that big old sheepdog of mine in the bedroom. Pavlik was already lighting my fire. He, me and a smoldering log. Snow in May was suddenly the best thing that ever happened to me.

A Ford Explorer with its bubble lights rotating, but no siren blaring, pulled to our door. As Pavlik went out to move his bike, I had an idea.

'Any chance I can catch a ride to my house with you?' I asked, following him.

He pushed the Harley over the curb cut and up on to the sidewalk. 'Are you done for the day? I thought you wanted to meet here at six.'

'I'm coming back. I just need to let Frank

out.'

'In a blizzard?'

'I promised him.' Deep solemnity in my voice.

To his credit, Pavlik didn't question a pact with my sheepdog. But then, Pavlik had met Frank.

'We can give you a lift there,' he said, 'but you're going to have to get back on your own.'

'Not a problem,' I said.

I stuck my head inside the store. 'Caron, Pavlik is going to drop me off at my house so I can let Frank out.'

She just looked at me.

'I promised.'

'Fine,' Caron said, after gazing momentarily skyward. 'But hurry, I have an appointment at one o'clock this afternoon.'

'I'll be back within the hour,' I said. 'Is Amy scheduled today?'

Caron shook her head. 'No, but she's on-call if we need her.'

Amy, our one and only employee, had been a great catch. Legendary, even. Multiply pierced and with rainbow-striped hair, she was the punked-out rock star of baristas, the bartenders of the coffee world.

Our star barista also was as out of place in

Brookhills on her end of the spectrum, as Sarah was at the other.

I glanced toward the waiting Explorer. The storm didn't show signs of letting up anytime soon.

'Other than additional people who land in our ditch, I can't imagine we'll have many walk-ins this afternoon,' I said. 'I doubt we need to bring Amy out into –' as I held the door open, I gestured toward the avalanche of flakes – 'this.'

'I agree, assuming you're here before I have to leave for my appointment,' Caron said, with an arched eyebrow I'd come to know and dread.

'I'll be back, Mom.'

'By twelve thirty.'

'Not a minute later.'

Caron played grouch. 'If I don't see you by half-past, we'll fly the flag at half-mast. *And*, I'll have to call Amy to help me.'

Subtlety did not come easily to my business partner. It was only after I climbed into the back of the squad that I realized if our land line was out, as Jacque had reported, Caron wouldn't be able to call Amy. Hopefully for Caron, she'd brought her cellular to Uncommon Grounds. Hopefully for Amy, she hadn't.

Pavlik closed the vehicle's door behind me, leaving his principal squeeze caged in the rear seat alone, while he took the front passenger one. I didn't recognize the female deputy who was driving.

'I'm Maggy Thorsen,' I said, unable to stick my hand through the divider between us in order to shake on it. 'Thanks so much for the ride.'

She nodded. 'My pleasure, Ma'am. Where to?'

I gave her directions and settled back as Pavlik got on the radio to let his office know he was on the way in to what, given what I was seeing, would probably prove to be chaos.

The snow was blanketing not only the ground, but the trees and shrubs as well. Absolutely beautiful, but destructive to the plant life that was, foolishly or bravely, already starting to bud, even blossom.

The overhead lines were hanging low from the weight of the sodden stuff clamped on to them. No wonder we'd lost phone service. It would be a miracle if the electricity didn't go as well, before this was all over.

As we pulled in front of my house, I saw that the daffodils were already buried under the snow. I might have had a chance to glimpse the tulips, which were taller, if the white-tailed deer that roamed the area hadn't eaten the Dutch beauties the moment they started to bloom.

Red, white – it didn't matter. The only tulips the deer left alone were the yellow ones, because I suspect they mistook them for daffodils.

Dumb deer.

And dumber snow, I thought as I climbed out of the squad into it.

THREE

Jake Pavlik rolled down the squad's window to talk to me. 'You're going to have to shovel this driveway if you're going to get your car back into the garage.'

I barely glanced at the foot-plus already covering the asphalt drive. 'My car's on the blink, and I plan to leave it in the repair shop until the thaw cometh.'

Pavlik 'blinked' himself, maybe because of the wind-blown flakes landing on his long dark lashes – the kind we women are never born with – or maybe, just maybe, because I had finally confounded him. 'Then how are you going to get back to the store?'

'Walk.' I was busy digging the house keys from my purse.

He shook his head. 'Not a good option.'

'Oh? And what would you suggest?' I was hoping for the offer of a ride.

'Got a sturdy set of cross country skis?'

So much for my taxi service.

'Or maybe put Frank to work as a sled dog.' Pavlik's eyes were luminescent blue as he chucked me playfully on the arm.

Mush, mush.

I tried to salvage the tender moment by thinking about Pavlik and the fire later that night, definitely sans sled dog or sheepdog.

'I suppose we could—' The cruiser's radio squawked, interrupting him.

I stepped back from the passenger window. 'I'll be fine. You go. Just pick me up in front of Uncommon Grounds at six.'

And with that, he *did* leave. Damn him.

'I'll call you before I come,' Pavlik called out the window.

I started to tell him the store phone line was out and he'd have to call my cell, but he'd already rolled the window up against the storm and was back on the radio.

Oh, well, Pavlik had been elected sheriff by a majority of the voters in our county. He'd figure it out.

I slogged up the driveway, registering the fact that the thunder, which seemed to wane as we drove, had gotten louder again. Mounting the porch steps to the door, I put the key in the lock just as a particularly loud BOOM-CRACK sounded.

As if the lightning from whence the thunder came had hit something.

As the sound echoed and then reverberated at double the first crescendo, I turned my key. Cracking the door open so Frank wouldn't mow me down like he usually did, I heard a panicked whimpering, followed by a thud-thud-thud.

Poor Frank. I couldn't even imagine what damage, psychic and otherwise, had been done to him. Besides having a full bladder, the sheepdog hated thunderstorms.

'It's OK, Frankie,' I called, like some demented doggy-mommy. 'I'm coming.'

I traced the pathetic whining to my bedroom and found Frank half under my bed. Actually, that's not technically true. The only part of him that fit under the bed was his head.

'C'mon Frankie-boy,' I crooned. 'It's OK, Mommy's here.'

God, sometimes I appall even myself.

Frank did his best to back out, but his big furry head and my slippery hardwood floor were combining to defeat him. As he struggled, the bed, which had been in the middle, walked itself steadily across the room. The 'thud', of course. And the feet of the bed had etched long scratches into the wood of the floor.

'Wait, Frank,' I ordered. 'I'm going to lift up the bed. You pull your head out.'

Frank's stub of a tail wagged.

'One, two, three,' I counted, as I slipped my hands under the box spring and pulled up.

Success. Frank skittered out from under the bed, landing me on my butt and sending scads of under-bed dust bunnies scudding.

Nature isn't alone in abhorring a vacuum.

'You big lug.' I hugged Frank. 'You're not a puppy anymore. You can't hide under the bed.'

Frank cocked his head, as if to ask exactly where he was *supposed* to hide.

As I considered the point, another boomer hit. Frank jumped and landed in my lap, shaking like a 110-pound leaf as the thunderclap rolled.

When it finally ended, he climbed off me, looking slightly embarrassed. Padding over to the corner, he paused and looked even more ashamed.

'Aww, Frank,' I said. 'Did you piddle?'

'Piddle' was a euphemism, not to mention a huge understatement. Frank's puddle of piddle could cause localized flooding.

I mopped up the pee with a roll of paper towels and, stuffing them in the trash bag, checked the clock. Eleven fifty-eight and I'd told Caron I'd return by twelve thirty.

I went to the door and opened it to let Frank out. He stuck his nose into the storm and swiveled back to me as if to say, 'Are you crazy?'

Then he turned and padded away disinterestedly. I suppose it was possible that, given the lake he'd created inside, he no longer felt the need to go *out*side. I hoped it didn't become a habit. I'd be forced to buy one hell of a litter box.

Beachfront property available.

'I have to leave, Frank,' I told him. 'But I'll be back at six.'

He was following on my heels now, the closest to herding behavior I'd seen the sheepdog actually do.

I pulled my Columbia jacket off a hanger in the closet, grabbed my boots and took the 'glove basket' down from the shelf. The first pair I pulled out were Ted's old ski-gloves. Then Eric's orange and yellow 'Big Bird' mittens. The ones that only a four-year-old, infatuated with *Sesame Street*, could love. And a mother would keep.

Eric was nineteen now. Perhaps it was time to purge the glove basket.

I chose my black gloves and hoisted the

basket back up on the closet shelf. As I did, one of the Big Bird mitties dropped to the floor. Frank immediately picked it up and started to whimper.

I knelt down and patted him. 'I know you miss Eric. I do, too. But, just think, it's already May. He'll be home right after exams.'

Frank seemed skeptical. I hoped he didn't know something about my son's studies that I'd managed to miss.

'And,' I said, going for cheery, 'I'll be home in just a couple hours.'

More skepticism.

'OK, six hours.'

Frank let out a huge sigh. Then, as if I'd asked for it, he padded over to his piddle place and poured me a new one.

'Now *that* was uncalled for,' I said.

God knows how I'd raised a child. I could not even control a sheepdog.

Another crash of thunder sent Frank skidding back to me.

'What am I supposed to do?' I asked him. 'Take you with me?'

He ran to the door.

I opened it, thinking he had to go out. You know, pee for a third time.

But Frank wasn't going anywhere without

me, apparently. Nor, if he had anything to say about it, was I going to go anywhere without him.

He stood crosswise at the top of the porch stairs, blocking my way until I relented and got the leash. Then he pranced up to me.

'You're not supposed to be at the store,' I said. Then, hoping that Frank wasn't current on Wisconsin business law concerning partnerships, I tried: 'Caron will fire me.'

Frank rolled his eyes. I know, because his eyebrow tufts twitched.

I checked my watch. After twelve. Caron was already ticked because I'd been late this morning. 'I promised to be back by twelve thirty,' I told Frank.

He danced at the top of the steps, happy to let me secure the leash for the walk. With a reluctant glance at the puddle he'd made and that I'd left, I secured the door and followed.

Despite his fear of thunder when he was in the house, Frank seemed to take it in stride during our walk. Me, I wasn't taking anything in stride. More like half-strides, with a dose of stumbling for good measure.

The snow was getting deeper. Maybe I'd call my neighbors when I got to the store and see if their son Petey could come over and shovel. In fact, I'd do that from my cellphone right now, if I could see the tiny screen in front of my face.

With the wind whipping and the snow falling in curtains, I could barely tell where I was going. Happily, Frank seemed to know and I just rode his tail, hoping he wasn't going to pull me off my feet and drag me for a block or two. Pavlik had been right. I should have used a dog-sled, à la the Iditarod race in Alaska.

The sidewalks were impassable, so we were walking along the shoulder of the road. We were on Brookhill Road, mere yards from Uncommon Grounds, when a car came careening around the corner from Civic Drive. The driver saw us at about the same time we saw him, I thought, but he just kept on coming.

I tugged frantically on Frank's leash and the two of us dove into the ditch. Too late, I saw that the car was barreling along, in our tracks and nipping at our heels.

FOUR

It was only when the car sailed over us and came to a halt about fifteen feet away that I realized not only were we in the ditch that Jacque had slid into earlier, but it was the very same Peugeot that was sharing it with us.

As Jacque climbed out of his re-stuck vehicle, he snarled something in French. It wasn't 'sacre bleu!' but I'd take bets that it was *something* 'blue'.

Frank and I got to our feet, Frank taking longer because he had four of them. Plus the fact that I'd landed on top of him. Poor furry thing had the wind knocked out of him.

'Slow breaths, Frank,' I said, scratching him behind one ear as he dragged air into his lungs via shallow gulps. 'You'll be fine.'

Frank looked at me, his expression a mixture of doubt and accusation.

'I didn't mean to land on you,' I said. 'Besides, you should blame—'

'What is it that you are doing on the road?' Jacque demanded.

'Trying to walk,' I said. 'As you may have noticed, there are no sidewalks anymore.' I looked around. The road was disappearing pretty fast, too. 'You nearly killed us.'

'It is you and your bear, you come out of nowhere,' Jacque said. 'You make me to slam on the brakes and –' he made a down and up gesture with his hand – 'poof! My baby is in the ditch again.'

'He's a sheepdog,' I protested, wondering what kind of pets the French kept on-leash. Elephants? Dancing bears?

But Jacque ignored me. 'And how am I to remove the Peugeot now?'

It was a good question. The tire tracks of the squad car that had come for Pavlik were already filling up with snow. There wasn't another car to be seen on the road – or what was left of it.

'I'm starting to think none of us is going to get out of here tonight,' I said. 'Including your car.'

The fishmonger shook his head wordlessly. Then he climbed out of the ditch and, with as much dignity as he could muster, stomped through the deep snow toward Uncommon Grounds. Frank jumped to follow, pulling me with him like I was attached to the rope tow on a ski slope.

By the time we reached the store, Jacque was already seated at the table he'd been sharing with Rudy when I'd left. Not that it mattered who Jacque was sitting with, since he was scowling blackly out the window.

Rudy cleared his throat from the table. 'Umm, could I get some more coffee maybe?'

'Coming right up,' Caron said, pointedly looking up at the clock above the coffee bean bins. Twelve forty.

'I'm sorry, Caron,' I said, leading Frank in and closing the door behind us. 'But we—'

'What in the world?' Caron was gaping at us.

Glad she was showing concern for our being nearly obliterated, I explained, 'Jacque slid off the road again and nearly hit us.' I patted Frank on the head, dislodging a haphazard crown of snow.

'I don't care about your adventures,' Caron said. 'I'm talking about *that*.' She pointed an accusatory finger toward Frank who, despite sitting respectfully, did seem to be melting all over the floor like the Wicked Witch of the West.

'Not to worry,' I replied hastily. 'I'll clean

it up.'

Caron tossed me a roll of paper towels. 'It's not just the slush he's making, Maggy. We can't have a dog in here. It's against the health department's rules.'

'I'll put him in the service hallway,' I replied. 'Frank's afraid of the thunder.' As I said it, a muted crash, followed by a long rumble sounded.

Frank peed, supporting my argument, but not exactly helping his overall cause.

'Get that dog out of here!' Caron shrieked.

Gotcha. Sheesh, Caron was strung tightly today.

I escorted Frank in back, but not all the way into the service hallway. Instead, I found some burlap bags, the kind they ship raw coffee beans in, and made a bed for him in the storeroom.

'You take a nice nap,' I told him. 'And if Caron comes in here, pretend you're a rat.'

I bucked out my front teeth and raised my hands, fingers apart so the nails would seem like claws.

Frank did three turns around the burlap bed and lay down facing the wall. I'd been dismissed.

Taking off my sodden jacket, I hung it on a hook on the back of the office door and looked down. Caron had been so busy reacting to Frank's presence, that she hadn't scolded me about not taking off my boots.

Too bad, because now as I slipped out of them, I stepped right into the puddle of dirty water they'd left on the floor. Served me right, I thought as I stuck my wet sock-feet into the tennis shoes I kept at the store.

When I returned to the front of Uncommon Grounds, Caron was wiping up after my boots. And Frank.

Rudy still had an empty coffee cup in front of him.

'Let me guess,' I called over to him, 'you're in even greater need of more coffee?'

When he nodded, I checked a timer on the pot. 'This was brewed more than thirty minutes ago,' I told Rudy. 'Why don't you let me start a fresh pot?'

Rudy raised his hand. 'Not necessary. The stuff in the barbershop sits all day.'

Jacque roused enough to concur. 'It is true. His coffee, she is very, very bad.'

'Well, then this should be "very, very good" by comparison,' I said, pouring Rudy a cup and taking it to their table.

They'd chosen the draftiest spot in the place, along the windows and adjacent to the door. However, it did give a spectacular, if gloomy, view of the storm.

I circled back behind the counter and rubbed my arms. A latte seemed just the thing for this kind of weather. I took out the skim milk and dumped some into a stainless steel pitcher, before sliding it under the frothing wand and turning it on. As the milk steamed, I tamped espresso into two porta-filters – handles with small metal baskets attached for the grounds. Twisting them on to the machine, I flipped a switch over each one and the dark brown espresso started trickling down into the shot glasses below.

As I dumped the shots into a latte mug, I looked over at Caron, who had moved on to straightening the runner in front of the door.

'Can I make you a latte for the road?' I asked, thinking about her appointment.

Personally, I thought she was crazy ventur-ing out into the storm, but I had something of a 'glasshouse problem' there, given my insistence on trekking home to let Frank out.

'I'm not going,' Caron said, proving she was either smarter than I was or that my tardiness had pushed her so late that she would have missed her appointment anyway. 'The office called me on my cell just after you left and said they were closing at noon today. And Sophie texted to ask if I could post a "Closed For Snow" sign on The Bible Store. Apparently, nobody in their right mind is out and about.'

I think Caron meant it as a slam to me, but I was busy digesting the fact that Sophie Daystrom, well into her eighties, text-messaged. Next thing I knew she'd be on Face-Book. MySpace. YouTube. eHarmony. Octa-genarians R Us.

Before I could get my head around all this, a frigid wind blew through the store. In the doorway stood what might have been a Yeti, but was, in fact, even scarier.

Sarah Kingston. And she was in a snow-covered snit.

'Are you OK?' Caron moved forward, her roll of paper towels cradled in the hollow of her elbow like a hunter carrying a shotgun. Caron seemed concerned, but I thought her private agenda was to catch Sarah – and the two inches of snow on her – before the real-estate broker could stray off our rug.

'OK? Do I look "OK"?' Sarah snapped, channeling Sophie Daystrom from this morning. 'It's a frickin' nightmare out there.'

'You didn't make it to your office?' I kept the coffee pot between Sarah and me. For my protection.

'I made it, but a helluva lot of good it did

me. The power is out. No lights, no heat. *You have power.*' She was looking at me like I'd struck a deal with the devil. Or at least the ghost of Thomas Edison.

I decided the best defense was a good offense. 'We should call the TV station and complain. A correct forecast would have prepared us for this.' Like venturing out with boots and a coat, instead of sneakers, a T-shirt and jeans.

'You'll get Aurora fired,' Caron said. She'd given up trying to keep Sarah on the rug. In fact, my partner looked like she'd given up on everything important to her as she slumped into a chair.

Sarah shrugged and joined Caron at the table. 'Doesn't matter. She's on her way.'

FIVE

'On "way" you say?' Jacque snorted. 'It is truer than you know, I believe.'

Again, I wasn't sure what he meant, but Rudy chose that moment to get up, pull on his coat and leave. As the door closed behind him, I heard the plaza's big John Deere snow-blower start up.

'Is Aurora on her way here?' I asked Jacque, but he just laughed harder.

Sarah regarded him suspiciously. 'No, Maggy. I meant "on her way" out of a job. I heard Aurora is getting the boot from TVR. The age thing.'

'The...?' Caron straightened up and pushed back her blonde hair. Excuse me, the 'Vibrant Blonde' hair that just last month had been 'Radiant Red' and, for the forty-four years before that, brown. Lower case. 'Aurora's not old.'

'That, my dear, is in the eye of the beholder. Or, in this case, the eye of the station

47

manager.' Sarah nodded at Caron. 'New hair looks good, by the way.'

'Midlife crisis color job,' I contributed. 'But blonde or not, Caron is right. Aurora can't be more than – what, thirty-five?'

Aurora – prophetically named by her parents after the meteorological 'Aurora Borealis', otherwise known as the Northern Lights – had been quite a bit younger than Way when they married.

Way continued to like them young. And petite, blonde and blue-eyed, judging from the women he'd run through both pre- and post-Aurora. And maybe *during* Aurora, for all I knew.

A lot of that went around in Brookhills, trust me on this one.

Sarah shrugged. 'Even thirty-five is old for television, especially now that "high definition" is here to stay. Besides, weather sluts need to be tiny, with perky breasts. Aurora is still tiny, but lately her boobs are flying at half-mast.'

I snickered, earning a glare from Caron, who I knew was considering having her own puppies hoisted. She gestured toward Jacque, who seemed to be transfixed by a copy of *Who Moved My Cheese?* from our bookshelves.

'There's more to a woman than a pretty face and perky breasts,' Caron said indignantly.

I thought about pointing out that if Caron really believed that she could save herself thousands of dollars in hair dye, Botox injections, and 'surgically-enhanced' tah-tahs over the next few years. But, no: in our town, growing young is half the fun.

Speaking of Brookhills' Barbies – they of the expensive SUVs, plastic faces and legs hinged at their wasp-like waists – one of them had pulled up in a Lincoln Navigator.

Given the thing was the size of a garbage truck – which is what Brookhills uses to plow its streets – I guess I shouldn't have been surprised the vehicle had gotten through the snow storm.

The Barbie in question climbed out, stepping down into a drift. Which particular doll we'd drawn was difficult to identify, since the fur-trimmed collar of her coat was pulled up to protect her face from the blowing snow as she approached and finally yanked open the door.

Fur. Blowing snow. In May. Even accompanied by a thunder-and-light show, it just wasn't right.

'Aurora is an educated woman. A meteorologist,' Caron said, getting up to serve the arriving customer.

'Yeah, well "the meteorologist" got it wrong.' I pointed out the window. 'Aurora said the snow was supposed to stay south of us, centered over Chicago. We were going to get just rain up here.'

'Apparently you missed this *morning's* forecast.' The customer folded down her collar and stomped her boots, sending newly crusted slush flying.

Aurora Benson smiled her best weather-slut smile. 'The line of demarcation between the snow and rain moved farther north than I anticipated last night. We can expect another ten inches of wet, sticky snow by tomorrow morning. Maybe more.'

'Great.' I was wondering, all of a sudden, how Pavlik, Frank and I were going to get to my house. Even if the snow stopped and the Harley could make it through the snow, Fat Boy was not going to accommodate a man, his moll and her faithful dog.

'If you have a radio,' Aurora said brightly, 'you can tune into 88.6 and our Weather Center will keep you up to date.'

Aurora 'Bore-ye-all-of-us' (forgive me) was already getting on my nerves. To the point I wanted to smack her one. And steal her SUV.

A long rumble of thunder sounded as the lights in the store flickered.

'Thundersnow,' Aurora said. 'A true meteorological rarity.'

I threw Caron and Sarah a satisfied look. I knew my Milwaukee micro-climate facts.

'And because it's just barely cold enough to snow,' Aurora continued authoritatively, 'the water content in the snow is very high. When the heavy, wet snow falls on the electrical wires, it clings. Eventually the weight of it...'

The lights flickered again, hung on by their toenails for a second and then went out. The 'O' on the readout of the battery-powered coffee-bean scale was the only bright spot in the dim room. We might not have a radio, but electricity or not, we'd be able to weigh our raw material. Couldn't use our grinder or brewers, of course. Or the cash register. Or running water, for that matter, since the pumps that brought it into the store were also electric. But then, given the white-out beyond the windows, we wouldn't be getting any sane customers anyway, so why worry?

A whoosh followed by a hum signaled that

someone had fired up the emergency generator.

As the cacophony of beep-beep-beeps coming from the assorted electrical devices that now needed to be reset started, Aurora slipped out of her coat and laid it over the back of a chair.

'I need to find Way,' she said. 'Do you mind if I leave this here to dry and go through the service hallway?'

'Not at all,' Caron said, eying the splotches of dirty slush coming off the bottom of Aurora's coat and landing on Caron's clean floor. 'Do you know when the snow will be cleared from our parking lot?'

Aurora sighed. 'The snowplow driver quit, so Way called me, trying to track down Oliver to snow-blow the parking lot.' She nodded toward the sound of the John Deere outside the window. 'I didn't know where he was, but apparently Way found him.'

God forbid either parent should know the whereabouts of their seventeen-year-old son.

Recalling Frank's odd reaction to the name of his master-in-absentia, though, I wondered if this was another omen. I made a mental note to call Eric at school, see how he was faring.

'Are the Twin Cities getting snow?' I asked Aurora, figuring I should get full value out of tolerating her here. Eric attended the University of Minnesota's flagship campus in Minneapolis/St. Paul – the Twin Cities to most of us and just The Cities for Minnesotans.

'No. This storm is centered around the Great Lakes. Your son, Eric, goes to school in Minneapolis, doesn't he?' She sounded wistful, like she wished her son was off to college, instead of cutting his high-school classes in order to hang around a strip mall.

'Sophomore year,' I said. 'He loves it.'

I said it because it was ... well, what you said to other parents. The truth was, though, that I really *was* a little worried about him, even pre-Frank, the Canine Clairvoyant.

Final exams were imminent and Eric seemed to be getting increasingly tense and maybe a little depressed. I tried to ask him about classes and girls and all that college shtick, but he'd get irritated with me. Said I was checking up on him.

I was, of course, but he wasn't supposed to trip to it so readily.

The snow would be a great excuse to call and see how he was.

'Oliver is thinking about Minnesota,'

Aurora said. 'Or maybe LaCrosse or Madison.'

University of Wisconsin in Madison was Wisconsin's flagship school. It was also tough to get into. Eric had good grades in high school and tested well, but he had been waitlisted at UW, before opting for Minnesota instead. I didn't think Oliver's grades were any better. In fact, I was pretty sure they were worse.

'Has Oliver applied?' I asked Aurora of her son. 'He's a senior, right?'

'He is, but Way wants him to take a year off. He says Oliver needs to get some "life experience" before he goes off to school.'

I was all for life experience, but I had a hunch that what Way really wanted was an indentured servant – one who could work at the mall full-time during the coming year.

Which reminded me: 'Is Oliver going to snow-blow the whole parking lot? That will take forever. Why did the snowplow guy quit?'

A cold wind whistled through the store, signaling the front door had been opened again.

'Way didn't pay him,' Aurora said. 'Honestly, if I'd known it was going to be even more of a pain in the ass to be that man's business partner as it was to be his loving wife, I would have forced him to sell Benson Plaza to a developer, taken my half and run.'

There was a gasp at the door, which made us all turn to the sound.

SIX

Gloria Goddard, owner of our little mall's pharmacy, stood just inside the shop. Snow covered her thin shoulders like 'a mantle of white', though she didn't look like she was feeling the whole *Winter Wonderland* vibe of the song.

And who could blame Gloria, or Mrs G as I thought of her? It was *May*, for God's sake.

'Goodness, Gloria,' Caron exclaimed. 'You must be freezing. Why didn't you come through the back hall?'

'The lights were off,' Mrs G said, hugging her arms close to her body to warm up. She apparently had been as prepared as I was this morning when she'd made the trip in to open the pharmacy and lunch counter. Mrs G was wearing what my mother would have called 'a house dress' and was clutching a white plastic bag.

Caron – God bless her, rising above the 'no snow in *my* shop' mantra – brushed at the older woman's shoulders, sending the accumulated flakes to the floor below. 'They were off only for a few seconds. Way must have fired up the generator.'

'It's spooky to be alone in the hall, even with the emergency lights on. I don't go back there.' Mrs G shivered, but she was looking steadily at Aurora, registering everything Way's ex – and our weather slut – had said. 'Are you talking about selling the mall?'

Aurora looked uncomfortable. 'I told Way that's what we should do. It would be a whole lot easier and cheaper than the current plan.'

'What *is* the current plan?' I asked. 'Way hasn't said much about it.'

'It is the gross national produce,' Jacque said from his table. He didn't sound happy about it.

'You mean "product".' Caron corrected. English wasn't Jacque's first language, so I thought it was cruel of a former advertising copy-editor like Caron to chide him.

'No, he doesn't,' Sarah Kingston said. She looked fairly dry, except for the bottom of her baggy trousers. Whether it was the depth of the snow or the 'wicking' effect of the hems dragging through it, her pants were wet up to her knees. 'Gross National Produce is a store. Or, more accurately, a chain of *super*stores.'

Ahh. 'They have one in Minneapolis,' I said. 'Eric was telling me about it. The place is huge, with individual stands of produce and bakery, meat and fish, prepared foods—'

'It sounds like our farmers' market,' Mrs G interrupted.

The Brookhills Farmers' Market was held in the parking lot that stretched between the police department on one side and the town hall and the adjacent fire station on the other. The newest structure is the fire station, which was built to replace the one that was burned down.

Long story.

The Farmers' Market always started the first Saturday in May, which meant the Public Works Department and Mother Nature, along with mother's little helper (the sun – what were you thinking?), had tomorrow to get rid of the snow.

The market was a popular, even mandatory, weekend stop for most of Brookhills, not just for the produce and plants and flowers, but also for the socialization. I love the market, even if I suspected that some of the produce had been purchased bulk at grocery wholesalers instead of grown on local back-forties. The corporate stickers on the 'homegrown' apples seemed a dead give-away.

'Gross National Produce *is* a Farmers' Market, I guess,' I said, 'but one on steroids and open twenty-four/seven.'

Mrs G, who ran the market, looked even unhappier. 'But what will happen to ours?'

I wasn't sure anyone knew that right now, but I tried to reassure her. 'I find it hard to believe people will want to stroll through a mall instead of outside in the sunshine.' God knows we had to do enough of that November through April in Wisconsin.

Oh, and on this year's May Day, as well.

Mrs G brightened a bit and I turned to Aurora. 'Is this thing going to occupy the whole mall?'

That was the vital question, of course. Uncommon Grounds was on the far end of Benson Plaza and didn't take up much of the mall's footprint. Maybe we could co-exist with Gross.

Memo to file: come up with a less insulting shorthand for the behemoth, just in case they did end up our neighbor.

But Aurora nodded to the 'whole mall' question and my heart dropped. Did the woman realize her gesture had functionally sounded my shop's death knell?

Aurora was peering out the window. And every time she saw a flash of lightning or heard the rumble of thunder she nearly clapped her tiny, weather-slut hands in meteorological joy.

'Shouldn't you be out reporting the storm?' I was being ornery, but, in my view, I was entitled. Aurora's predictions about Gross had stolen my thundersnow. Or at least my ability to enjoy it.

'I'd love to be,' she said, holding up her cellphone. 'But the towers must be down. I'm not getting a signal, so I can't get an assignment, either.'

That statement was greeted by the sound of simultaneous flip-phones, like Captain Kirk had just decided it was time for all of us to call Scotty and have him beam us up.

'No signal,' Caron said, flipping hers closed.

'One bar,' Sarah offered. And then: 'No, no, wait. There it goes. Nothing. *Nada.*'

Damn. That meant I wasn't going to be able to call Eric today.

I filed it away under *other* things to worry about and turned to Sarah, who knew everything 'real estate' going on in Brookhills.

'Back to Gross. Who's the owner? And why would Benson Plaza want to kick out well-established tenants to gamble on one, big-box store?'

Sarah shrugged, but I knew her plain face well enough to realize she was holding back. She glanced over at Aurora, but no answer came from the Weather Slut, either.

Jacque shrugged. 'The owner? She is our own Naomi Verdeaux. And for your "why", Miss Maggy, you must ask Way. It is he, after all, who is shtupping my former wife now.'

Another intake of air. Not quite a gasp, like Mrs G's earlier at the door, but noticeable nonetheless. This one came from Aurora, still by the window. Instead of addressing Jacque's comments, though, she turned her attention back outside. 'Ooh, look at all that lovely precipitation.'

Talk about your oxy-moron.

For my part, I wanted to get to the root of this shtupping. 'Jacque, let me be sure I understand. Way and Naomi are...?'

'Doing the dirty,' Jacque confirmed. His French accent made it sound almost classy. *Doing zee dir-tee.*

'But why?' Caron asked in astonishment. 'Way is even older than you are.'

Sarah, across the table from her, rolled

both eyes. Though Caron was 'even' older than Jacque's thirty-nine, my partner had proven susceptible to the lure of younger men in the past.

Jacque stood up. 'I do not remain here only to receive the insult.'

'Yes, you do,' Sarah said flatly.

I looked at her. My blunt-spoken real-estate friend seldom forgot that there were potential clients under every rock.

Now Sarah got up and went to the door. She pushed it open. 'See?'

'See?' Jacque said. 'I see nothing.'

'My point exactly.' Sarah closed the door and went back to the table she shared with Caron.

I looked out through the window. There was a snow drift covering the ditch where Jacque's car had been. If there had been any chance of getting the Peugeot out – and I didn't think there was – it had disappeared. Along with Jacque's "baby".

I giggled.

'And what is so funny?' Jacque asked. 'It is because of you that I am in the ditch again.'

'And the bear,' I reminded him. 'Don't forget the bear.'

'Bear?' Mrs G gasped. Poor woman, I had unintentionally piled one worry on top of another.

Which didn't stop me from giggling again.

Then I put my hand on her shoulder. 'Not a bear, just Frank.'

Mrs G nodded, relieved. She knew Frank from the one time I'd attempted to bring him to the Farmers' Market.

For years, I'd seen Brookhills Barbies strolling the aisles with their poodles and their puggles – a 'revolutionary' new cross between a beagle and a pug. Personally, I'd have called the hybrid a 'bug'.

Anyway, Frank had taken a disdain to puggles and sat on one, according to the owner of the mutant involved. I just figured Frank was tired. He doesn't operate in 'Princess and the Pea' territory. Last week my poor sheepdog fell asleep with his rump on the porch steps and his head down on the grass.

For Frank's transgression, real or concocted, he had been banned from the market. Personally, I was just happy a police report hadn't been filed.

A sheepdog with a record.

Speaking of animals, I cracked open the door of Uncommon Grounds to see if Pavlik's Harley hog was still safe. And so it was, standing relatively unscathed under the plaza's eaves and our awning.

As I finished looking out, however, the door was yanked from my hands.

SEVEN

'Has anyone seen Way?' Rudy asked, snow cascading from the hood of his parka. 'Our esteemed landlord started the generator, but I think it may be running low on gas.'

As Jacque shot him an annoyed look and stepped out into the storm, Aurora said, 'I'm not sure, but I need to talk to Way, too.'

'Do you know where he stores the gas for the generator?' Caron asked. It was a fair question, since Aurora was as responsible for the mall as Way. If our pipes froze – or, for that matter, if *we* froze – it would be a hell of a mess to clean up for both of them.

'I don't bother with those things.'

Aurora said it in the same tone the CEO of my former company had once said to me, 'I don't remember names. PR people remember names.' I'd already grown tired of pulling the guy's corporate chestnuts out of the fire. That Christmas – the one just after Ted left me – I happily left them roasting and quit.

And I'd never looked back, though I had caught my checkbook register seeming wistful a couple of times.

'Good,' I said to Aurora. 'Then you can sit here and freeze your butt off like the rest of us.' As I said it, I had to repress a shiver. It really was getting cold and my jacket was soaked through.

Aurora rubbed her bare arms and looked at her coat hanging on the chair.

I put my hand on it. Misery loves company.

Aurora swallowed hard. 'Fine, I'll go look for Way and find out where the gas cans are located. Or Oliver, for that matter. He should know where they'd be.' With that, she exited through the back door.

I probably *should* have let Aurora take her coat, since Oliver, assuming he was the one clearing the parking lot, could be found by just following the sound of the snow-blower. Even as I thought it, though, the roar of the machine died. And it didn't sound like an easy passing.

'Uh-oh,' I said, as it first thudded, then gurgled and, finally, went silent. 'The John Deere must be down to fumes, too.'

'Good. That poor boy must be tired,' Mrs G said. She had been unusually quiet up to this point, sipping a cup of coffee she'd poured for herself. 'Oliver can't possibly clear all this snow on his own. His father should be ashamed. It's nearly three in the afternoon and the snow continues to fall.'

Gloria Goddard had to be pushing eighty-five, but she was still a beautiful woman. Natural grace and great cheekbones would do that for a person. Having a husband twenty years her junior might have helped, too. Mrs G was a 'cougar' before anyone had even thought up the label.

Sadly, though, Mrs G's husband, Hank, had died about a year ago, accidentally shot by a buddy while they were deer hunting in northern Wisconsin. Worse, it was the only trip in the space of the last two decades that Gloria hadn't accompanied her husband 'up north'.

'I may not be a great shot,' I remember Mrs G saying at Hank's funeral, 'but I *sure* as hell wouldn't have mistaken him for a deer.'

With Hank gone, Mrs G was left to run the pharmacy they'd started together. I knew that she was lonely, despite the attempts of those of us around her to provide some companionship. Thing is, daytime eventually turns into night. When Ted left me, I'd wake up at 2 a.m. every morning. The loneliest hour in all the twenty-four, when the fresh start of dawn seems a lifetime away.

The one silver-lining for Mrs G?

Oliver.

He and Mrs G had bonded, maybe because being Way and Aurora's son created its own version of loneliness. Oliver had grown up around the mall, reading comic books at the pharmacy while eating balanced meals – if peanut butter cups and Pepsi are counted in the new food groups. When Mrs G got wind of that, she'd taken him under her wing and become a surrogate grandmother.

I wondered how either of them would survive without the pharmacy.

For now, though, Mrs G was still the mom of the strip mall. 'I brought you candles from the store,' she said, standing up and digging into the plastic bag imprinted 'Goddard's Pharmacy'.

'These,' she held up two candles in the shapes of apples, 'are close-outs from Christmas. Cinnamon, I think. And these –' she had a handful of small metal boxes – 'are off the cosmetics wall. I think you pack one in your suitcase when you're on the way to a cheap affair. They smell like a whorehouse.'

'That has my name written all over it,' I said, grabbing a couple of the metal boxes.

'Same here,' Sarah said, taking two for

herself.

Mrs G gave her a suspicious look. 'Wait a minute. You're not a tenant here.'

Sarah seemed affronted. 'My office is right down the street. We lost electricity, too.'

Mrs G grabbed back the boxes. 'Then you buy your own candles. What do you think I am? The Red Cross?'

Sarah stood down. Nobody in Brookhills with any brains at all got into a pissing contest with Mrs G.

'I'm heading back to the pharmacy,' the older woman said, rolling up the leftover candles in the plastic of the bag.

A ding at the door and I turned. Geez, we should have a blizzard every day. It was good for business. On the other hand, nobody was paying for their drinks. A classic Catch-22.

Or $4.95 for a latte.

The new arrival was a woman I'd seen around but without a formal introduction. I'd sure heard about her, though.

Naomi Verdeaux folded back the hood of her fur coat. 'I'm so glad you're open. I've been circling, looking for Way Benson. I think there might be a dim light on in his office, but nobody answers my knock.'

'We're on the generator,' I said, 'so you might have seen the automatic emergency lights. I don't think we've met. I'm Maggy Thorsen.' I stuck out my hand.

'Of course,' Verdeaux said, pausing to tug off thin leather gloves one finger at a time before shaking hands with me. 'Way has told me all about you.'

'Really? Like the details of our lease and when it expires?' I asked pleasantly as I poured her a cup of lukewarm coffee. The generator was just barely keeping the lights on now. There was no way it could heat the water so we could brew more coffee or even keep the crappy stuff already in the pot hot.

'That's not nice, Maggy,' Caron said, taking the cup out of my hand and extending it to Verdeaux. 'I'm Caron Egan. I think we met at Christ Christian.'

Christ Christian, you might recall, is the big church up the street from my house. Anyone who's anybody belongs to it. I don't, which I guess tells you something right there.

Verdeaux waved aside Caron's coffee offer. 'No, thank you, and please don't apologize. Your partner is right. To be honest, Way did show me your lease. It was necessary for our negotiations.'

I heard the back door close and turned to look for Mrs G, but she already had disappeared into the service hallway.

Like Aurora, Verdeaux was a PB-EB – petite, blue-eyed blonde. She turned to Rudy, who had shrugged out of his parka, for support. 'As town chairman, I know you advocated the idea of a "destination" shopping experience. Our project will be a boon to Brookhills.'

I wasn't sure that the inhabitants of Brookhills needed – or even wanted – to become a 'boon town'. It seemed to me they were happy to be left to themselves. Sort of like Switzerland, except snootier.

Rudy preened. 'I did. And I expect that Way, to whom I passed the baton, will implement these initiatives.'

Before Verdeaux could answer, Sarah chimed in, 'An upscale organic food store can only be good for Brookhills. It's a wonderful idea.' She was gushing and the Sarah I knew didn't gush.

I cocked my head toward Naomi Verdeaux, but spoke to Sarah. 'Client?'

'Hope so,' she said, passing me to get to her potential pot of gold. 'I don't know if you recall, but I'm Sarah Kingston. I worked with Jacque when he opened Schultz's.'

'Of course,' Verdeaux said, sticking out her hand. 'Good to see you again.'

'Same here. And if there's anything—'

'Wait a second,' I interrupted. Jacque Oui was known only as Brookhills' fishmonger to the stars, reigning over the seafood counter at the small specialty store. 'If Jacque's the owner, then why is the store named Schultz's?'

Verdeaux looked at me. 'What *were* we supposed to call it, Oui's?'

'Or Oui-Oui's?' Sarah contributed, and they started cracking up.

'Maybe Oui-Oui-Oui?' Verdeaux offered. 'All the way home?'

Now both exploded in laughter. They'd be rolling on the floor any minute.

I decided to leave the two women to their bonding.

'I think I'll go look for Way and Oliver, too,' I said.

Still giggling, Sarah and Verdeaux just waved their hands at me. Caron eyed them uncertainly, as though she wasn't sure what the joke was and wouldn't be comfortable joining in until she did.

I stepped out into the hall and closed the door.

EIGHT

Once in the rear hallway, I was stabbed by a frigid blade of wind. Damn, I must have been in such a hurry when I took the trash out earlier that I'd left the outside service door open.

From our shop's back door, you could turn left and travel down the inside of the 'L' to the other businesses in Benson Plaza. If you turned right, though, you could exit into the secondary parking lot, where the extra spaces and trash dumpsters were. The arrangement made it very handy for us, though we often stashed the plastic garbage bags in the hall anyway, to dispose of later.

I shivered in my thin T-shirt, wishing I could wave a wand and magically dry my soaked Columbia jacket. Caron and I had decided not to take up precious storage space with a washing machine and dryer for towels, but the dryer portion sure would have come in handy now.

In fact, I'd be tempted to hop right in there with the jacket. Not that the generator had enough juice to power such a thing. It was barely keeping the lights on.

Moving carefully to my right, I concurred with Mrs G. It was spooky in the dim hallway, especially with the sounds and sights of the storm emanating from the open door just twenty feet away like something out of *The Twilight Zone*.

Storms involving thundersnow sound differently than regular electrical ones. The falling snow muffles the thunder and the low clouds seem to hold the sound close, usually creating more of a long, menacing growl than a sharp crack.

As I got to the door and reached for the handle to pull it closed, the lightning strobed above. I stopped to look at the way the bolts, which I couldn't see, reflected off the clouds. First here, then there, then back here, then over there. It reminded me of the scene in the movie *Close Encounters of the Third Kind*, when the alien space ship is hovering above the clouds before making itself visible.

'Dum dum dum, hoo-hah.' I was trying to recreate the musical tones from the film, the ones the scientists played to invite the ship to land. When hummed into the teeth of a raging storm, however, the sequence of notes turned out sounding ... well, just plain 'dum'.

Anxious to get back inside Uncommon Grounds and warm – not to mention safe from extraterrestrial life forms – I tugged on the door handle to close it. The thing would not budge.

Of course. There had to be snow in the way. I tried to clear it with my foot, but it was frozen slush and awfully heavy. I needed a shovel, but I didn't see one in the hallway.

As the light show continued to flash above, I looked to the far right and caught sight of the big John Deere snow-blower. I didn't know how to run the monstrosity, but lying in front of it was what looked like a half-buried shovel. Good thing the John Deere hadn't run into it, the collision between the auger – the blade that goes around and chops up the snow – and the shovel probably would have been the end of both.

I tugged again at the door. Damn. Much as I hated to shovel, I'd left the door open and that made it my responsibility to get the thing closed to keep in what was left of our heat.

Trying to stay as dry as possible, I gingerly took a step toward the shovel and sank to my knees in snow. Well, no need to be careful anymore. Best to get out and back fast, the five-second rule on dropping food on to your kitchen floor, but now applied to avoiding frostbite.

I waded to the shovel and gave it a pull. I could barely see in front of me, but I stubbed my toe on something hard. Probably the scoop of the shovel buried under the heavily packed snow. I gave another yank, and it gave a bit.

But just a bit.

This was ridiculous. I was soaked up to my waist, but I wasn't going to leave without that damn shovel. Sort of a sword-in-the-stone thing.

My hands were frozen and the handle was slippery. As I leaned down to get a better grip, the lightning above me lit the snow at my feet.

Screaming, I toppled on to my butt, making an impromptu snow angel. Then I scrambled to my feet as fast as I could, wiping my hand on my jeans.

What I had thought was the end of a shovel nearly buried in the snow was instead the handle of something like a hatchet or cleaver.

Buried in Way Benson's back.

It wasn't that, though, nor the blood on my hands, that made me scream. I'd seen more than one body. Even held a grisly murder weapon or two.

No, what scared the shit out of me was the red sunburst around what little was left of our landlord's head.

NINE

Back in Uncommon Grounds, Caron was the first to offer a theory. 'Maybe the snow-blower's auger got stuck and Way tried to clear it?'

'With his head?' Sarah snarled. She was pouring bottled water over my hands so I could wash them, the emergency generator no longer up to the task of keeping the pump running and our plumbing working.

For my part, I was trying not to gag, either at the cooling, sticky blood remaining on my hands or the image of Way, his head blown open like a surreal chrysanthemum blossom on the lean stem of his body.

'You're sure it's Way Benson?' Caron asked me. 'You could be wrong, right?'

'Wrong,' I said, flatly. 'Unless there's another six-foot-four Clint Eastwood look-alike running around with "Aurora" tattooed on the back of his neck.'

'Or *not* running around,' Sarah contributed dryly, capping the bottle of water.

We'd left Way out there because I knew that's what Sheriff Jake Pavlik would want: preservation of a crime scene. Still, it seemed wrong. Still, yet, though, I sure as hell wasn't touching him again.

When I'd screamed, Caron and Sarah had come running, followed by Rudy Fischer and Naomi Verdeaux.

After the requisite gasping and gaping, I'd gotten hold of myself and told Rudy and Verdeaux to find Aurora and tell her what we'd found. I thought she should be the one who broke the news about Way to Oliver, who, after all, was still their son. I also asked my messengers to round up anyone else still stranded in the mall and have them gather at our coffee shop.

To be honest, though, I wasn't sure if I was rounding up the 'usual' suspects or circling the wagons of potential victims.

Most likely, it was neither. I'd simply seen too many movies.

'Sarah's right,' I finally managed, drying my hands a little too vigorously with a paper towel. 'Way didn't get his head accidentally stuck in the snow-blower, any more than he stabbed himself with ... whatever he has sticking out of his back.'

My words were punctuated by a rumble of thunder. Under the circumstances, more ominous than usual.

Caron giggled, a little hysterically, I thought. 'Our own sound effects.' She began reciting, ' "It was a dark and stormy night—" '

'Not to mention goddamned cold and snowing,' Sarah interrupted. 'We won't be out of here until spring.'

'This *is* spring,' I reminded her. 'But I see your point. I can't imagine we'll be able to leave the mall tonight. It's already getting dark – night dark, not just snow dark.'

Six o'clock had come and gone with no sign of Pavlik. Not that I really expected him, given the weather and his myriad responsibilities in an emergency. Even calling me was out, since the phones – including the cellulars – were, as Jacque put it, 'dead'.

Join the club.

'We might as well face it,' I said with a sigh, 'we're stuck here until someone plows us out.'

Sarah had been studying me. 'You're as happy as a pig in shit, aren't you?'

'About what?'

'Another murder, but this one all to yourself.'

That was unfair, I thought. 'It's not like I go looking.'

'You don't have to. They come to you.'

'Death Makes a House Call.' Caron was still chuckling. 'It could be a movie.'

Caron has always had peculiar ways of dealing with stress. I try not to judge, but it ain't easy.

Loud voices from the service hallway signaled the troops were gathering. I stepped out into the corridor. I knew everyone would want to see, but I needed to make sure Pavlik's crime scene stayed intact.

Aurora led the way toward me, with Mrs Goddard, Naomi Verdeaux and Rudy in single file behind her. There was no conversation amongst them that I could hear. Trailing were Luc and Tien Romano, the father/daughter team who owned An's Foods. Unlike the other four, Luc and Tien were walking next to each other, talking softly, even reverently.

Tien Romano's name reflected her looks and ethnic heritage, just as her father's reflected his. Tien was a beautiful mix of her Italian–American father and An, her Vietnamese mother.

I knew that Luc and An had met when Luc was stationed in Saigon during the Vietnam

War. An was dead when I'd met Luc, but I knew from her picture, displayed in a position of honor above the cash register, that Tien had gotten the best of both her parent-worlds: complexion and facial features from her mother, thick, curly hair from her father. Finally, while the tilt of Tien's eyes was An's, their hazel color was Luc's.

In short, Tien was a beautiful woman and I'd caught myself wondering why she still hadn't 'found someone'.

Then I internally slapped myself upside the head.

Why did a woman have to be with a man to be fulfilled? God knows that marriage to Ted hadn't been so 'ful'.

When Aurora reached me, I laid a hand on her shoulder. I wasn't quite sure what to say. I knew that despite my divorce and his betrayals, I would feel awful if something happened to Ted, both for myself and for Eric.

I wasn't sure what Aurora's reaction was going to be. By the look on her face, she didn't either.

I settled for: 'I'm sorry, Aurora. Have you been able to find Oliver?'

She shook her head. 'Where is he?'

I sensed that she wasn't talking about her

son. 'In the back parking lot, just to the right of the service door.'

As Aurora moved forward, I cleared my throat. 'It's pretty bad. Are you sure ... are you sure that you want to?'

She met my eyes. 'Either I see him now or I imagine what it looked like for the rest of my life. I guess I prefer the known to the unknown.'

Having seen Way in the flesh, or what was left of it, I wasn't so sure Aurora would continue to feel that way. But I understood, nonetheless. I'd probably have decided to do the same, against all advice.

Aurora opened the door and stepped out. The others followed and looked around questioningly, mostly at me.

I pointed.

In the short time since I'd found the body, an amazing amount of additional snow had fallen. The blanket of flakes I'd dislodged when I pulled on the 'shovel', was nearly replenished. Using the John Deere as my signpost, I led the group toward Way's body.

The blood spray was still discernible, the warm blood melting the snow under it, creating an almost embossed effect.

Aurora put her hand to her mouth and for a second I thought she was going to be sick.

As I moved forward, though, she waved me off.

'Do you have any idea what happened?' Her voice sounded calm. Or maybe the tone of shock.

I decided straight answers – what I had of them – were best.

'There's something stuck in his back. You can see the handle ... there.' I pointed. 'I think someone may have come up behind him when he was snow-blowing and attacked him. Then, when he fell—'

'He went under the auger of the snow-blower?' This last was from Oliver, who had pushed his way to the front of our group. Apparently, the boy had finally arrived to help his father. A bit late.

Oliver was always pale from too much time spent inside, but he looked even more so now in contrast to the green-plaid flannel shirt he wore. As he looked down at the body of a parent who'd pretty much ignored him, his face took on the same cast of his shirt.

I wasn't sure what to say, but that was probably best left to Aurora, anyway. Until I noticed that she hadn't so much as glanced at her son.

Accordingly, I answered Oliver's question like I'd answered his mother's: the best I could. 'I don't know, but it's possible.'

Since the John Deere was positioned with its auger-end toward Way's head, his son's assumption seemed logical. My only question was whether our landlord fell or was pushed forcibly enough to land under the spinning blade.

'What's that in his back?' Rudy said, stepping to the front of us.

The whole group was getting closer and closer, one person maneuvering past another like a game of cautious, macabre leapfrog. I strode back into the lead and held up my hands.

Jacque, whom I hadn't seen arrive, peered around me. 'I believe it to be a cleaver, for the cutting of meat and bone.'

Nauseatingly put, but I had to admit it had looked like a cleaver to me, too. Since Luc Romano had been a butcher by trade, though, I didn't want people speculating. That was my job.

Besides, something told me you could chop heads off fish with a cleaver, too. 'I thought you'd left,' I said, irritably, to Jacque Oui.

'I go around the corner to the pharmacy. There they have the flashlights and the batteries.'

'And radios.' Mrs G held up a banana-yellow transistor model that certainly went for at least fifty bucks when I was a kid and now probably could be had for more like a buck fifty. Burgeoning technology – the antidote to inflation. Unless, of course, you wanted *new* technology. I understood you could get an eight-track player for pennies on eBay. *With* cartridges.

Mrs G twisted the radio's dial. '...calling this bizarre spring snowfall the storm of the century. All of Milwaukee County and Brookhills County services are shut down and people are being ordered to stay off the streets. Electricity is out in a wide area covering western Milwaukee and eastern Brookhills and crews are not expected to be able to reach the downed lines until the snow stops. That, we're told, may not be before tomorrow morning. When all is said and done, certain sectors will have received up to three feet of snow.'

Holy shit.

I looked down at my knees. A good eighteen inches was soaking through my jeans already. Preoccupied with Way's murder and people's reaction to it, I hadn't really felt the cold. Now I looked around and saw that Oliver's lips were blue and trembling as he hugged himself for warmth. Even as I thought it, Mrs G came over to add her body heat to his.

Only she didn't look any warmer and suddenly I was freezing, too. 'OK, there's no reason to stay out here. We can talk about this just as well inside where it's warm.'

'Or at least warmer,' Tien said, rubbing her arms.

Tien managed the store for her father, who ran the meat department. There, meat cleavers hung like the animals they butchered from fixtures on the wall. Thing was, though, Luc had been selling off his equipment, including the cutting tools. Anyone could have one.

'Didn't you buy a set of knives from Luc?' I asked Caron as we moved inside. 'They have those rough, wooden handles, right? Like all knives and cleavers used to have?'

'Like the cleaver in Way's back?' Caron shook her head disgustedly. 'As a favor between friends, could we get sucked into just one murder where you *don't* suspect me?'

Luc caught up to us as I pulled open the door to Uncommon Grounds. A good-natured guy, Luc came by his trade naturally. His mother had owned a deli throughout his childhood and he'd continued the tradition with An's. He was a teddy bear of a guy, though this teddy bear still had the muscles.

Luc had built them back when he was in the service and maintained them in the years since by whacking meat at the butcher counter. I refused to believe he was whacking anything else anywhere else.

'Maggy,' Luc said now, 'Gloria has a wood-burning stove in the corner of the pharmacy and we managed to get it going before we heard about Way. I think we should all move in there for warmth.' He hesitated. 'And besides, maybe it would be a good idea to put some distance between us and –' he gestured toward the outside door – 'that.'

'Good idea.' Not only for Aurora and Oliver, but for everyone else as well. For the first time, I thought about Naomi Verdeaux. Aurora might be Way's ex-wife, but Verdeaux was Way's current ... whatever.

I tried to view Verdeaux sympathetically. For about ten seconds and then gave up. I had a lot of trouble generating any emotional connection with the bitch who was going to destroy not only Uncommon Grounds, but the other stores in the mall as well. Not that Way was blameless. Maybe his double-dealing was the reason I was able to – despite the horror of it all – separate myself from the man's murder.

I wanted to know who killed our landlord – not because of Way, himself, but because of the people who would be affected by his death. Oliver. Aurora. And … well, I wasn't sure how many more would be affected negatively. Would Way's death save the mall? I wasn't sure of that, either. Worse, I didn't know if I wanted to be sure.

'Maggy?'

I started. Luc stood waiting.

'Sorry,' I said, closing the door to Uncommon Grounds. 'I was thinking about what I could bring over food-wise, to share. We should have muffins left over from breakfast and maybe—'

But Luc waved me to calm down. 'Don't bother. Gloria has the lunch counter and I'm right next door with plenty of food.' His eyes darkened. 'In fact, it'll be a good way to clear out some of our stock.'

'Are you looking at space for another store?' Sarah had come up behind us. 'There is a new shopping plaza going in near Poplar Creek. I'm sure they'd love to have An's as a tenant.' She looked at me. 'And Uncommon Grounds.'

'Thanks,' I said, 'but the scuttlebutt is that Poplar Creek already has a Starbucks signed on.'

'Where'd you hear that?' Sarah was obviously affronted at the thought that something could go on in the Brookhills real-estate realm without her knowing about it.

'Amy's my source,' I said. 'And you have to be aware that *she's* aware of all things coffee.'

There was no arguing with that, even from Sarah. She did, however, start patting her pockets, reflexively looking for a smoke.

'C'mon,' I said to my friend. 'We're going to Goddard's. Gloria has a wood stove.'

Sarah didn't look all that interested in a stove, wood or otherwise. 'I'm going to talk to Rudy. He'll know what building permits have been approved.'

'Only up to the election last month,' I called after her as she strode ahead of us.

Sarah ignored me and I turned to Luc. 'Sooo, you were saying you might open where?'

Luc smiled sheepishly. 'To be honest? Maggy, I'm not sure what we're going to do. Tien and I have done the shop-keeping gig for a very long time. Maybe it's best that she's free to follow something else. Something Tien wants to do, rather than feels she *has* to do.'

'I never got the impression Tien was unhappy,' I said.

Tien was walking ahead of us, talking with Rudy. Her father seemed to tighten.

'She says she's not,' Luc said in a clipped tone, 'but my daughter's young. She shouldn't still be working with her father.'

We watched Rudy say something to Tien, before he broke off from the group and ducked inside the barbershop's back door. Probably avoiding Sarah, who had been on his heels, but now continued on.

Tien dropped back to us. 'Rudy says he has a surprise and asked me to grab some things from the store. Is there anything else we need?'

'I'll go with you,' said Luc, voice back to normal. 'I'm going to pick up some bottled sodas. I don't think the fountain at the pharmacy will work without electricity.'

The two of them disappeared into An's as Mrs G opened the door of Goddard's.

Jacque stepped past her into the store. 'I find the battery-powered lights. Like this.' He lifted what looked like a Japanese lantern and flicked a switch. The neon green lantern – complete with a serpent silhouetted on it – lit up.

'Are those party lights?' Caron asked, going to help with the multi-colored paper globes. 'They're so cute.'

Meanwhile, Mrs G turned, one hand on Oliver's shoulder. The poor kid still looked shell-shocked, and who could blame him?

'You all make yourselves comfortable now,' she said. 'I'll make us some nice sandwiches.' She looked at Oliver. 'Give me a hand?'

He nodded wordlessly and they disappeared into the kitchen.

As I said, Oliver looked like he was on the edge. Aurora, too, I was sure. It couldn't be easy seeing your son's father after he was Cuisinarted by a snow-blower.

Which reminded me of Eric and everything he'd had to deal with, father-wise. I hated not being able to check with him even by text message, which was his preferred method of communication – especially if he was trying to avoid questions. I'm a whole lot easier to ignore in cyberspace than I am in person.

Which gave me a thought. Cellphones might not be working, but perhaps a text message might go through. A couple of years back, I'd been caught in the aftermath of a steam-pipe explosion in New York City and tried to call Ted and Eric to let them know I was safe.

Even as I flipped the phone closed after several aborted attempts to get through, a text message icon popped up. The message, from Eric, read: 'r u ok?'

Eric later explained to me that texts didn't require as many 'bars' of reception as calling out does.

Despite that information stored in my poor brain's data banks, I hadn't tried sending a text.

Eric could run, but he couldn't hide. And neither could anyone else.

TEN

My cellphone was back in Uncommon Grounds, so I turned on my heel and went back out the door. The hall was quiet, since Rudy, Luc and Tien were still scouring their respective establishments for sustenance.

I'd forage, too, after I got my phone. There must be something Uncommon Grounds could contribute to the effort.

The corridor seemed even spookier than it had earlier, which wasn't a good sign. The last time I'd felt like this I'd stumbled on a dead body in five minutes flat.

Turning the corner, I was just passing The Bible Store, when I heard a thud.

This was both a good sign and a bad one. Good, because corpses don't thud. Bad, because murderers do.

According to Caron, The Bible Store had not opened today. Without a paid staff, the good-book store often suffered at the hands of undependable volunteers. Sophie Daystrom was the most faithful, but even she had surrendered to the weather today. Especially understandable, given the 'Hyundai' ransack earlier this morning.

But had someone else decided to pick up Sophie's slack?

I tapped timidly on the door. If someone was inside, I'd invite them to Goddard's for sandwiches.

No response, so I knocked a second time, even as the thunder – which had been quiet for a while – kicked up again.

Maybe it was thunder that I'd heard, not someone...

Another thud, followed by two more. Still no one came to the door, so I tried the handle. Locked.

If it *was* the bogey man, he was being awfully noisy. The alternative was that someone was inside and unable to come to the door. Maybe even injured.

I backed up and rammed into the door, using my shoulder like I'd seen on TV.

Damn.

That hurt. A lot.

I let out an involuntary whimper and rubbed my aching joint, hoping I hadn't dislocated something. For its part, the door hadn't budged.

Rather than risk further personal injury, I decided to grab my phone from Uncommon Grounds and then go back and find Luc. He was a big guy and a vet. He could probably kick the damn door down using just one big toe.

I hadn't locked the door of our coffee shop, so I went in and made a beeline for the office to get my purse and cellphone. As I picked up my bag, another long roll of thunder pounded the earth, this one seemingly right overhead. It was followed, uncharacteristically for thundersnow, by a loud crack.

Even as the sound died out, there was another thud like the ones I'd heard through the door of the adjoining store. As I stepped out of mine, the door of the storeroom swung open abruptly. I put out my hands to keep the door from smacking me in the nose. That successful effort, though, left me without a spare hand to regain my balance. I lurched against the wall and slid down, landing on my rump.

Frank sat down side-by-side with me and gave me a disdainful look.

'I left you alone when it was thundering.' Frank sniffed.

'I found a dead body,' I offered by way of apology.

But Frank was having none of it. He lifted his back leg and licked ... you don't want to know what he licked.

I said, 'Was that you thumping?'

Still no response. He just continued his ablutions, pretending I was invisible.

Now I know my sheepdog. Frank was punishing me or being evasive. Or both.

But why?

I pushed myself up and stepped into the storeroom to look at the back of the door.

A hole. A big one in the cheap, hollow-core door.

Like someone had thudded his furry sheepdog head into it.

I looked around the door at Frank. 'You put a hole in that.'

He switched legs.

I sighed, accepting my reprimand. 'You're right. I brought you here and then abandoned you. I –' hesitating to admit it – 'I even forgot you were here.'

Frank, who was nothing if not gracious, stood up.

'I'm sorry.'

Apology accepted. Frank jumped up with paws on my shoulders. Just in time, I saw the tongue.

'No kisses, no kisses!' I said frantically,

twisting my face away from his. I pushed him down gently.

'Do you need to go out?' I asked.

Frank's tail wagged and he pranced to the front door. I turned the latch and pushed, but got only about a two-inch opening. The piled-up snow was blocking the door.

Frank looked at me expectantly – urgently, even – and put his nose in the opening.

'Sorry, buddy,' I said. 'I don't think you're going to fit.' Made me think of that Bible verse about it being easier for a camel to go through the eye of a needle than for a rich man to get into heaven.

I might not be rich, but my canine camel sure as hell wasn't going to fit through this particular needle.

I sighed. 'I'll let you out back,' I told Frank, 'but Way's body is strictly off-limits.'

Frank didn't answer, but waddled to the hallway door. A doggy version of crossing one's legs.

I let him out into the hall and he made a beeline for the outside door.

'It's Pavlik's crime scene,' I said, figuring Pavlik might get more respect than Frank's owner would. The sheriff and the sheepdog were buds, after all.

Frank, though, didn't give a damn. He just

wanted out.

I turned the lock and pushed at the door. Since we'd all tramped out less than an hour ago, the snow was compacted enough for me to get it open.

Frank dashed out as I called after him, 'Remember...'

A door slammed behind me, followed by footsteps pounding down the hall. Before I could turn completely around, I was struck in the back.

ELEVEN

No blackness, no stars. I saw only white.

The snow, I realized after a terrifying moment. But . . .this white wasn't cold. Or wet.

This white was ... fuzzy.

Oh, for God's sake. 'Get off me, Frank.'

He shifted and I spat out a mouthful of dog hair. 'I'm OK, boy. Now ... get ... off ... me.'

Frank complied. He had laid himself diagonally across my head – presumably to protect me and keep me warm. I didn't think asphyxiation was on his radar screen.

Frank stood up, giving me a thankfully rare view of his underside and then moved off, managing to step on me with only one of his paws.

I sat up, flexing to see if I truly was 'OK'. My back, where I'd been hit, felt sore. Bruised, for sure, but if it had a cleaver in it, I'd know, right?

Unless I'd gone into shock.

Like the victim on television who doesn't realize there's a railroad spike through her skull until she overhears: 'If we remove the thing, it'll kill her.'

Which begs the question of how you accessorize a railroad spike if they *don't* remove it.

'Take a look.' I twisted around so Frank could see my back. 'Do you see anything? Blood? Maybe something sticking out?'

My devoted pet, who had been watching me with concern, perked right up and started bouncing around, obliterating the crime scene.

The first one, not mine.

I'd said 'sticking', not 'stick', but Frank was running away through the snow like a wide receiver going out for a long pass.

'We are not playing fetch,' I called after him, getting to my feet.

'Did you scare him away?' I asked as the sheepdog circled back. I was checking out my body parts one by one, making sure everything was working properly. I didn't see any blood on the snow, so I wasn't leaking anywhere. 'Did you get a good look at him?'

Frank didn't seem to have a clue and neither did I. Because I'd been staring out into the brighter snow, when I'd turned back to the dark hallway I'd only gotten an impression – like a reverse negative – of someone coming at me.

I had to admit, though, his silhouette seemed familiar. The way he moved, maybe, or...

An intruder?

I brushed myself off. I'd been assuming that Way's killer was either someone stranded in the mall or, better, an outsider who had killed him and fled.

Now I had to entertain the possibility that there was someone – maybe a stranger and maybe not – also hunkering down in Benson Plaza.

I shivered – not from the cold this time, but it *did* remind me that I was freezing. I rounded up Frank and we stepped back into the service hallway. Warmer, but not by much, and my clothes were now soaked through.

Since I assumed my assailant had escaped outside, I turned the lock on the door to the back parking lot to keep it that way. Then, returning to Uncommon Grounds, I sat down at the desk and rummaged through the file cabinet drawers, looking for something, *any*thing to wear. I came up empty, except for an Uncommon Grounds apron.

I held it up to Frank, who was sitting on the floor next to me, as close as he could get without being on my lap. The sheepdog projected the impression he wasn't going to let me out of his sight. I wasn't going to let him out of mine, either.

I stood up, holding my cellphone. 'Let's go see if Mrs G has something I can change into.' At the very least, word was that there was a fire in the wood stove. If I stood near it long enough, maybe I'd dry out.

Or toast like a marshmallow. Right then, not such a bad fate.

Frank walked me to the door. I opened it a crack and looked out. No sign of any bad guy, but then I didn't know what he looked like anyway.

Or even, to be completely honest, whether he *was* a 'he'.

In lock-step, Frank and I navigated the hall back to Goddard's. I had my hand on the sheepdog's back, fingers twisted in his thick fur. I couldn't shake the feeling that Frank might have saved my life.

Frank. The dog I'd reluctantly taken custody of when Eric left for school and Ted had just left our marriage.

I sniffled. 'Thank you, Frank.'

He grunted. Gracious, even in triumph.

As we navigated, I checked around to see where my attacker might have come from. So far as I could tell in the dim light, everything was the same as it had been when I'd approached Uncommon Grounds. When we reached The Bible Store, I tried the door.

Still locked, so 'he' couldn't have come from there.

When I arrived at Goddard's, I expected Mrs G to have the same reaction to Frank that Caron had earlier. Instead, she welcomed him with open arms. Sitting at the horseshoe-shaped lunch counter, I filled in everyone who was there – Mrs G, Caron, Sarah, Jacque and Aurora – on what had happened.

'You could have been killed,' Caron said, wringing her hands in a way I found oddly – but sincerely – concerned.

'No, no.' Jacque was shaking his head. 'There is no need for panicking. This person, he desires to make the great escape, not injure anyone.'

Easy position to take when you're not the 'anyone'.

'Maggy was lucky she had this dog,' Mrs G said, giving Frank a tummy rub. 'He probably saved her life.' She switched to Frank exclusively and cooed. 'Didn't you sweetie, huh? Didn't you, my good boy?'

Frank licked her face. I shuddered, but didn't tell her where that tongue had oh-so-recently been.

Oliver joined us just then. 'Hey! A dog!'

Frank padded over to him. Mrs G watched with a smile on her face and then turned to me. 'Your clothes are wet.'

I looked down at my waterlogged T-shirt and jeans. They were even worse than my jacket was now. 'Do you have anything here I could change into?'

Mrs G thought. 'I don't have much in the way of soft goods, but there might be a T-shirt or two in "Tourist Trash".'

'Tourist Trash?' I peered up at the aisle markers.

'I don't label it that,' she said, leading me to 'Souvenirs'. 'This seems to work just a tad better.'

Personally, I found the tourist trash approach refreshingly honest. And maybe the stuff by the cash register could be subtitled: 'Crap you don't need and wouldn't buy if you weren't stuck here waiting in line for so long.'

But sure enough, Mrs G was able to come up with a green 'Brookhills: Land of Hills and Brooks' T-shirt. It came down to my knees, but the shirt was dry and that, to me and my shivering torso, was all that counted.

'Now, what are you going to do for pants?' she asked, eyeing my wet jeans. 'I had pink sweats with "Brook" on one butt-cheek and "Hill" on the other, but I had to send them back last week.'

'The missing S'? I hazarded.

Mrs G nodded. 'No one takes pride in their workmanship anymore.'

Or spelling. Though leaving the 's' off Brookhills has proven to be a common mistake over the years. Why do you think our main drag is called Brook*hill* Road?

But, as wonderful as pink mis-spelled sweatpants sounded, I was still very grateful for the T-shirt alone. 'That's fine,' I said. 'My jeans will dry.' Eventually.

Mrs G snorted. 'Denim? That will take days. How about some nylon knee socks?' She was leading me to the magical land where pairs of pantyhose reside in small plastic eggs.

I wasn't hot on the knee-sock idea, but I did thumb through the display. 'Hey, how about opaque tights?' I said, pulling out an egg.

'I'd go with the black,' Mrs G said, casting a critical eye. 'They'll look better with the T-shirt.'

We couldn't find black tights in my size, so I chose navy ones to accessorize my green T-shirt. My feet were freezing, so I pulled on a pair of red tasseled slipper-socks.

I looked like an elf on holiday, but at that point I was beyond caring.

Luxuriating in my new-found dryness, if not exactly warmth, I went to stand by the fire.

Aurora was already there. She looked me up and down. 'Nice outfit. Besides getting soaked, are you hurt?'

I thought it was considerate of her to ask about my wellbeing when she had Way's death – and manner of death – to endure. 'I'm fine, Aurora. But, thanks. How about you? And Oliver?'

'Oliver? I don't know. He doesn't talk to me.' Aurora lifted her head. She had tears in her eyes. 'Doesn't *want* to talk with me.'

'It's epidemic at that age,' I said. 'I barely hear from Eric.' With a pang, I realized I hadn't tried to text my son yet.

Aurora managed a smile. 'So what next, Maggy? You've rounded up the usual suspects. Aren't you going to start interrogating us?'

If I had to have a reputation at this point in

my life, I'd rather that it be as a slut than a snoop. Still, we play the cards we're dealt.

'I admit I want to know who did this,' I said. 'Don't you?'

Aurora didn't answer the question. Instead: 'If you're looking for people who hated Way, it's a wide-open field. Despite his education, he is ... was, crude.'

'Crude?' I'd thought of Way as egotistical and self-centered, but not necessarily gutter material.

She laughed, bitterly this time. 'Did you know that he commissioned a tattoo in my honor?'

I did, because I'd seen it on Way's lifeless body.

'Well, that was romantic, right?' I said. I mean people don't have ink injected under their skin for just anyone. Unless they're drunk.

'Sure,' Aurora said. 'Until we divorced.'

'And then he wanted to have it removed?' I guessed. I'd heard lasers were effective, if not perfect, for tattoo removal.

'Removed?' Her laugh was not so much humorless as it was just plain tired. 'No, Way didn't have it lasered off. He just put a big X over it and had the name of the next woman tattooed below it.' Her voice faltered. 'And the next, and the next.'

Like notches on a gun or, probably closer, on a bedpost. 'You mean including...' I canted my head toward Naomi Verdeaux, who had just come in from the back hallway.

'I was on the back of his neck. He's worked his way south since then. She –' Aurora nodded toward Verdeaux – 'is on his butt. The man was a pig.'

Interesting. I wondered just how Aurora could know *who* was on Way's butt. 'You did marry him,' I reminded her.

'Even a pig can be charming,' Aurora muttered, throwing a look in Verdeaux's direction. 'In short bursts.'

Way's ex lowered her voice even further. 'Believe me, it doesn't take long to realize that Way was interested in only one thing: Himself. He was nothing but a back-stabber and...'

'Someone stabbed back,' I said.

Aurora froze for a beat, then nodded.

'But who?'

Despite what Sarah had said about my being happily snowed-in with a corpse, I wasn't liking this role very much. Funny how being attacked personally could take all the vicarious pleasure out of being trapped in a strip mall with a murderer.

'God, will you look at that coat?' Aurora said, as Naomi Verdeaux shrugged out of it by the lunch counter. We watched as Verdeaux hung the coat on a hook between the adjacent booths and moved away to talk with Sarah near the window.

'It *is* gorgeous,' I said. 'I mean, despite it being dead animals and all.'

'Sheared mink. With sable trimming, even the hood and cuffs. I was drooling over it at Saline's Fur Studio last fall.'

'It would look great on you.'

Aurora shrugged. 'Way probably bought it for her. Or, worse but typical, bought it for me, and then gave it to her. The little slut and I are the same size.'

'PB-EB,' I said, reflexively.

Aurora's eyes narrowed.

I bit my tongue, but did I let it stop me? Nah. 'Petite, blue-eyed blonde. It seems to have been Way's type.'

'You got that right.' Aurora sank into the booth next to Verdeaux's fur coat. 'You should add a Y to the acronym, though. Young was the primary requirement for Way.' She sighed, stroking the coat absently. 'Hell, for a lot of people.'

'Like your station?' I sat down across from her.

'My station?'

'The television...'

'Got it. Yeah, they say I "skew" old.' A grim laugh. 'That's in contrast with my ex-husband, who "screwed" young.'

Having had experience with a similarly cheating spouse, I figured I was entitled to crack a smile.

Aurora drummed her fingernails on the table. 'You know, it's hard enough to be replaced by a younger version of yourself at home. But on your job, too?'

'It sucks, on both counts,' I agreed. 'My husband dumped me for a younger woman, too.'

'Really?' Aurora canted her head. 'I didn't know that.'

'Well, we've never had much chance to talk before now.'

Aurora smiled. 'Once in a blue moon. Or every thundersnow, maybe. You doing OK since your divorce?'

I sat back in the booth, realizing. 'I am, in fact. It's good to be on my own, but Ted...'

'You still have feelings for him?'

'No, not really. He's a good guy – except for the cheating part – and he *is* the father of my son. It's just that Ted's had a rough go of it lately and I guess I feel sorry for him.'

'A dentist, right? Is business slow?'

'He's lost a few patients.' It was true as far as it went, but I didn't want to get into Ted's soap opera of a life right then with Aurora, a woman I barely knew outside a television screen.

'We reap what we sow,' Aurora said.

'Meteorological maxim?' I asked, trying to lighten her mood. Of course, with Aurora's ex-husband a frozen stiff out back, only so much levity was appropriate.

'More like retribution of biblical proportions.' Aurora changed her tone. 'Which reminds me, I want to make some observations on the storm. Maybe I can become the Wolf Blitzer of our thundersnow and save my job.'

I knew she was referring to the CNN reporter who had been coincidentally on the scene in Baghdad at the start of the First Persian Gulf War in ... God, could it be nearly twenty years already?

Sheesh, Aurora wasn't the only one skewing old.

The meteorologist slid out of our booth and stood up. She called to Mrs G, who was coming out of the kitchen, knife in hand. 'I'm going to need a—'

'Take whatever you want,' Mrs G said with

a flourish of her knife. 'I'll keep track and you can pay me when the power comes back on.'

I made a mental note to pay Mrs G for my 'ensemble' as Aurora went off to choose a 'Hello Kitty' notebook and matching pen ($9.43) from the stationery aisle. Before I could mentally tally my own bill, Naomi Verdeaux took Aurora's place across from me.

'Nice outfit.'

Verdeaux really was an age-regressed version of Aurora, right down to their cornflower hair and too-blue eyes. Where Aurora's eyes always seemed – whether by nature or professional obligation – open and friendly, Naomi Verdeaux's were empty. Even callous.

Robin's egg-blue eyes, transplanted into a shark. Like the predator had swallowed the poor thing whole and kept its eyes for its own use.

TWELVE

'I just came from the bathroom in the back hallway,' Naomi Verdeaux, aka the Great White, was saying to me.

Like I cared.

'It looks as if somebody is *living* here. Do you know anything about that?'

Over the last few months, I'd seen Mrs G's car parked in the back lot when I left at night. Most times, it was in the same space when I came in at five thirty the next morning. Did I suspect that she was staying in the store rather than going home to an empty house? Hell, yes. But it was none of Verdeaux's business.

'This pharmacy has been in our mall for decades. It wouldn't surprise me if Gloria and Hank have a lot of personal things stored here. I doubt we're experiencing the first night the entire plaza has been snowed in. Or maybe she's had to work late doing inventory.'

'Inventory?' Verdeaux laughed. 'I don't imagine it's even possible to *do* an inventory of the trash that's piled up in this place over those same decades you were talking about.'

Verdeaux leaned closer over the table between us, her tone now less confrontational and more gossipy. 'Know what I found in the high cabinet over the toilet?'

'Charmin. No, wait. Cottonelle.'

'Very funny.' Another inch of leaning toward me and I was going to bitch-slap her. 'A box of what looks like ammunition. And a dead squirrel.'

Stuffed, I hoped. The cabinet Verdeaux was talking about was nearly ceiling height. The despicable little snoop would have had to climb up on the toilet seat to reach it.

'Mrs G's husband was a hunter,' I told Verdeaux, as if it was any of her business. 'I'm sure she put those things up there so she wouldn't be ... reminded of earlier, happier times.' I didn't mention the revolver Gloria still kept in the cash drawer.

Verdeaux pursed her lips. 'There are probably lots of memories for her here after all these years. You, too.'

'Yes,' I said, wondering about the change in tactics. And tone. Now the woman sounded vaguely human.

Verdeaux tapped the table top with the nails on both her index fingers. 'I know that Rudy's barbershop was here first and Goddard's second. How long has your shop been in the mall?'

Give her this: she'd done her homework. Rudy had been the 'make-or-break' tenant – the one that put the mall at fifty-percent occupancy. Hitting that mark allowed the Bensons to refinance at a lower rate so they could afford to finish the project and begin another. And don't think that Rudy was above reminding Way of that every time the Barber of Brookhills wanted something. Rudy dearly loved having the upper hand, something Caron and I had never experienced.

'We opened Uncommon Grounds a little over a year ago.'

'Ahh, that's why your lease had already been renewed when I came to Way with my plan.' She began tapping those manicured fingernails even faster. 'Bad timing, that.'

Bitch, squared. I cleared my throat. 'So, you plan to take over our space, too?'

'Eventually, though that will have to be Phase Two.' Verdeaux smiled. 'The good news is that since you have it built out as a coffee shop, we'll just have to knock down the dividing wall to make it Gross National Produce's own, in-store cafe.'

Caron and I, along with our late partner Patricia Harper, had put countless hours of planning into Uncommon Grounds. The stainless steel counters holding the espresso machine and coffee brewers. The refrigerator tucked under the counter so we'd have milk for cappuccinos and lattes within easy reach. The Lucite bins that showcased twenty different types of coffee beans. The ceramic tile floor. The navy-topped tables and matching chairs. The condiment cart at the side of the door to draw people away and avoid traffic jams at the ordering counter.

'Wait a second,' I said, now leaning forward on *my* side of the booth. 'You're planning on kicking us loose and then using our shop as *your* café? Why not just let us stay?'

Verdeaux shook her head. 'It's not the Gross way, Maggy.'

'Not the "Gross ... way"?' I repeated disbelievingly.

A voice behind me said, 'Has it occurred to you, Naomi, that your "Way" is dead?'

I'd been so focused on the seemingly inevitable demise of Uncommon Grounds that I hadn't noticed Aurora rejoining the party. Now she plucked Verdeaux's coat off the hook next to us.

'Did he buy this for you?' Aurora asked the other woman.

Verdeaux looked confused. 'Way?'

'Yes, my ex-husband. Did you know that he and I were seeing each other again?'

It sure was news to me. But then, Brookhills seemed to have more layers than a wedding cake.

I slid sideways in the booth so my back was against the wall, legs stretched out on the bench and tasseled slippers pointed toes-to-the-ceiling. That way I could see both Verdeaux and Aurora without swiveling my head like I was at a tennis match.

Despite the news, I wouldn't have described Verdeaux as all that upset. 'No, Aurora, I didn't know that. But it doesn't surprise me.' She smiled. 'I believe you catch more flies with honey. And Way did, too.'

'*Honey*, believe me,' Aurora said with a matching smirk. 'I'm certain *you've* caught more bugs than a Venus fly tramp.'

I barely contained my 'atta-girl' fist pump. Since I wasn't sure which of these titans was going to win the battle of Benson Plaza, I didn't want to piss either of them off. On the other hand, my heart was with Aurora.

And she continued, 'You're not a stupid

woman, Naomi. You must realize that, with Way gone, I'm the one – the only one – who'll be making any decisions about Benson Plaza.'

As Aurora spoke, the door into the hallway opened and Luc and Tien joined us. Luc was carrying two packs of soft drinks and Tien had an orange, a bottle of something I didn't recognize and a jar of maraschino cherries.

Curious. But I had other entertainment.

'We have an agreement,' Verdeaux said.

'Way and you *had* an agreement.' Aurora shrugged into Verdeaux's coat. 'A verbal one or –' she gave Verdeaux a wink – 'should I say oral? But, either way, it's not binding on me.'

'That's my coat,' Verdeaux sputtered. 'And what else would you do with this mall? The tenants have been evicted and I'm sure they've made other plans. Perhaps even signed leases for space elsewhere.'

Verdeaux looked to me. Then at Luc and Tien. And, finally, toward Mrs G and Oliver, who had just come out bearing plates of food. 'Right?'

Well, no. But Aurora didn't give me or anyone else time to answer. 'So maybe I'll just sell the land to a developer.' Way's ex shrugged. 'There's a hotel chain that's just *dying* to get their hands on it.'

Geez, this was going from bad to ... well, immeasurably bad.

I raised my hand. 'Umm, I can stay and I think—'

Aurora interrupted me. 'Now I'm going to go out and measure the snowfall, so I have data when I finally get out of this place and on the air.'

She stared down at Verdeaux. 'My coat is at Uncommon Grounds. You don't mind if I take yours, do you?'

Verdeaux looked very much like she minded. Apparently, though, she was still counting on the honey/fly thing. 'Of course not. Be my guest.'

I watched as Aurora slipped her pad and pen into the pocket of the coat and pulled the sable-trimmed hood up.

'Thanks ever so much,' she said, giving the front door a shove with her hip. The door, which faced a different direction than Uncommon Grounds, must have had less snow piled up against it, because it swung open. Either that or Aurora was in lots better shape than me. 'We can talk more when I get back.'

And, with that, Aurora was gone, leaving us shivering in her wake.

'Will somebody pull that door closed?' Luc asked, as he went to set down the packs of cola and lemon-lime soda. 'The wind is keeping it open.'

Caron went and tried. 'It won't stay shut.'

'Turn the lock, so it latches,' Sarah suggested, as Mrs G began bringing out plates of sandwiches. 'We won't have any trouble hearing Aurora when she comes back.'

'Wait.' I had been so engrossed in the catfight that, when Aurora stormed out, it hadn't occurred to me that she was not only storming into the storm, but also, potentially, into the clutches of my recent attacker.

I went to the door and turned the lock so I could re-open it.

Sarah gave me a dirty look. 'Caron just locked that.'

'And Aurora's out there, maybe with a bad guy.' I stuck my head out. The icy flakes stung my eyes, but all I could see was snow, punctuated by the occasional flash of lightning. 'Aurora?' I called into the night.

Only a ragged report of thunder answered. And, in my elf costume, I was hardly dressed to go out and look for her.

Luc came to my side. 'What makes you think the killer is still nearby?' he asked. 'If I were him, I'd be long gone.'

I looked at Tien's father. I didn't think Luc had killed Way, but if I was wrong, he might be trying to throw me off. Or not. Besides, Luc was huskier than the guy who had knocked me down. I thought.

God, this stuff gets confusing.

'I would've thought he wanted to get away, too,' I said. 'But apparently not.' I filled him in on the attack.

'Even more reason to keep buttoned up,' Sarah said, taking the door away from me in order to close it and turn the deadbolt. 'Better to keep the killer outside.'

'But not us *in*, apparently,' I protested. 'Aurora isn't in here, safe with us.'

'Her choice,' Naomi Verdeaux said with a shrug. She not only didn't give a rip about Aurora, but she didn't seem all that worried about her own coat out in the snow. Of course, the animals had lived in the snow when they were alive, so why worry about them when they're dead and warming your new arch-enemy?

'It's OK, Maggy,' Luc said in a low voice. 'Aurora is no fool and, besides, what I said about the murderer goes double now. He knows you saw him, and I can't believe a sane man would come back here.'

Unless he wasn't sane. Or he was coming back for me. A chill ran down my back and it had nothing to do with my flimsy outfit.

'I'm going to go wash my hands before we eat,' Verdeaux said abruptly, sliding out of the booth we'd shared.

Eat. I glanced over at the lunch counter where the sandwiches awaited. I was really, really hungry. For not the first time in my life, food took precedence over my more noble impulses.

'There's no running water,' I started to remind Verdeaux, but she was already out the door to the back corridor. I wanted to wash my hands, too – what with the blood earlier and the sheepdog more recently. Maybe some soap from the shelves and bottled water, if we had more...

'Take some of that waterless hand cleaner.' Mrs G pointed toward the rack of impulse purchases by the cash register. 'Only ninety-nine cents plus tax.'

I grabbed a little blister-packed bottle. 'Great idea. I'll use some myself and take the rest to Verdeaux.' I was working at getting the plastic safety-seal off the bottle as I approached the door to the hallway.

It swung open, and I jumped back. Frank, still shadowing Oliver, barked.

'A little jumpy, are we?' Sarah asked.

An understatement if I ever heard one. I wondered if the Goddard pharmacy section was still stocked. A little Valium was sounding real good to me all of a sudden.

'Sorry that took so long.' Rudy was brandishing a bottle of brandy. 'I couldn't find where I'd put the new bottle of Korbel.'

He was talking about the brandy, not the champagne. Apparently a barber doesn't have a desk drawer to keep his booze in like any respectable office worker.

'Booze,' I said, stepping aside to let Rudy in. 'Thank God.'

'Is something wrong?' he asked, looking around.

'Besides Way being killed and Maggy attacked?' Sarah said sarcastically. 'No, everything's peachy. Why do you ask?'

Rudy turned to me, surprised. 'Wait a second. You were attacked? When? Are you OK?'

I wanted to explain, but egg salad and disinfected hands were calling me. 'They –' I waved at the rest of the cast of *Survivor: Strip Mall*, as I stepped out the door – 'can fill you in. I have to hit the bathroom.'

'There's no water.' Rudy's voice followed me. 'You'll...'

I didn't hear the rest of it as the door closed behind me. Without the benefit of Goddard's fire and the lanterns, the hallway seemed pitch-black and arctic, even with the emergency lights.

Trying to sublimate my fears – big word for futile task – I felt along the wall for the bathroom door. As I reached for the handle, it sprang open, bashing me in the forehead.

'My apology, Maggy,' Jacque's voice said. He grabbed my arm to steady me. 'I did not see you there.'

'I'm OK,' I said, though I was still seeing fireflies in the dark. I had a feeling 'fear of doors' was going to join my other neuroses. A-door-aphobia. 'I was looking for your ex-wife. She said she was going to use the bathroom.'

'I did not see my ex-wife. I am afraid –' even in the dim light I could see the sheepish look on his face – 'that you may not want to go into the restroom just now.'

That would explain why I hadn't seen Jacque for a while. He'd been stinking up the bathroom. And the toilet wouldn't flush, of course, without running water. Ugh.

'Here. Clean your hands.' I gave him the hand disinfectant and went back into Goddard's.

THIRTEEN

Luc, Tien, Sarah, Oliver, Caron and Rudy were all sitting at the lunch counter when I returned. I took the empty seat at the far end next to Sarah, and Oliver set a heavy white plate sporting an egg salad sandwich, dill-pickle spear, and pile of potato chips in front of me.

At seventeen, Oliver was almost as tall as his father Way who, when he had his head, was well over six feet. In contrast to Way's rugged looks and dark coloring, though, Oliver had his mother's blonde hair and blue eyes.

'Thank you. This looks great,' I said just as Jacque came through the door. He was followed by Naomi Verdeaux.

'I find her,' Jacque said. 'She is not in the bathroom. She is in the mall office.'

'Why ... what were you doing in Way's office?' Rudy asked, looking surprised.

Verdeaux shrugged and took a seat next to

126

Luc. 'Using the bathroom, of course. Some-body –' she looked at Jacque – 'was in the process of stinking up the other one. I see that, at least, hasn't changed.'

Verdeaux didn't get a rise from her ex-husband, but she did from Oliver. 'Where'd you get a key to my father's office?'

I thought Verdeaux had the grace to blush, but it may have been the reflection off the pink lantern light taped to the wall next to her. 'Well, I—'

'God!' Oliver put his hands to his head like he thought it was going to explode. 'My father was always such an asshole.'

No one seemed to have anything to say to that. I tried, of course. 'You might not know all the facts,' I said. 'I mean, maybe Ms Ver-deaux and your father were just ... umm, friends.'

I looked around. 'Right?'

Rudy lifted the bottle of Korbel. 'Brandy old-fashioneds, anyone?'

Even to old-timers, a brandy old-fashioned sweet – Wisconsin's classic drink – might seem an odd pairing with an egg salad sand-wich, dill pickle and potato chips. Still, unusual circumstances call for unusual cocktails.

Rudy and Tien mixed the drinks. Using a

'Welcome to Brookhills!' shot glass from the tourist trash aisle ('That's $4.99,' Mrs G said, tallying it.), Rudy measured out the brandy. He spooned a teaspoon of sugar into a Flintstones' jelly-jar glass, added a dollop of bitters, the brandy and a rapidly melting ice cube from Goddard's freezer. Then he topped it off with Luc's lemon-lime soda before passing the drink on to Tien, who garnished it with a cherry and an orange slice speared on a toothpick.

Since I was on the end of the counter, I got the first one. I sniffed. Typically a wine-drinker – and with just enough knowledge to be obnoxious about it – I would normally turn up my nose at the state's flagship concoction.

Today, though, it smelled like nectar of the gods. Whether my God, or somebody else's, I didn't care. I took a sip and moaned. 'This is heaven. Thank you, Rudy.'

He nodded. 'I know it's a bit ... old-fashioned,' he chuckled at his own joke, 'but they are comforting.'

'Like tomato soup and a grilled cheese sandwich,' Caron agreed, downing hers.

'Or tuna noodle casserole,' Mrs G offered, old-fashioned also in hand.

'McDonald's cheeseburgers and orange

drink,' Oliver said, sticking his hand out for a glass.

Tien hesitated and looked at Mrs G. Oliver was under-age, but Mrs G nodded and I concurred. 'I don't think he's going to be driving anytime soon,' I said, looking out at the still-falling snow. I was starting to get worried about Aurora.

When we all had our drinks, Rudy raised his glass. 'To Way,' he said.

'Why?' Caron asked and promptly hiccupped, covering her mouth with her hand. She'd finished her first old-fashioned, then managed to filch another. And she was half-way through the second.

'Because he's *dead*,' Sarah said. 'It's a tradition. Suck it up.'

Caron popped the cherry into her mouth. 'Way was a womanizing two-timer,' she managed around it. 'And we all know it.'

I raised my eyebrows at her and cocked my head toward Oliver. 'His son is here.'

'It's OK,' Oliver said. 'My father wanted to get rid of the mall, which is the only place I ... I...' He looked at Mrs G.

'Belonged,' Tien finished for him. 'I can understand that. Basically, I grew up here, too.'

Her father, who hadn't touched his glass,

looked like he wasn't certain he should be proud of the fact his daughter had matured in a strip mall. Judging by the way Tien had turned out, I didn't think he had anything to worry about. 'I'm going to get some more lemon-lime soda and fixings,' Luc said. 'We need anything else?'

'More brandy,' Caron said, raising her glass.

'Your father wasn't a bad man,' Mrs G told Oliver after Luc had left. 'He was just all ... business.'

'So was Mr G,' Oliver said, 'but he didn't kick people out of their homes.'

Verdeaux, who had been busy stirring her drink, caught that. 'Are you living here?' she asked sharply.

Mrs G flushed, or so I imagined in the dim light. 'I stay some nights,' she admitted. 'I work late and there's nothing to go home to, so...' She shrugged.

'Gloria doesn't have a home,' Sarah whispered in my ear. As she said it, the wind whipped up outside, causing the plate glass windows to creak.

'What do you mean?' I whispered back.

'The bank foreclosed on their house. In addition to being a hunter, Gloria's husband Hank was a bit of a gambler. She had to take

130

out a home-equity loan for his funeral and to pay off his debts. She managed to keep things afloat for awhile, but then...' Her shrug matched Mrs G's.

Sarah's information fit with what Naomi Verdeaux had found in the bathroom, as well as with what I'd witnessed car-wise in the parking lot. All that wasn't enough to make me feel less guilty about not being more attuned to a friend who needed help.

'If I had my say,' Oliver injected as Luc came back in, 'no one would have to leave. I'd keep Benson Plaza just the way it is.'

'I'll drink to that,' Caron said and hiccupped.

It was going to be a long night.

I took a slug of my drink and surveyed my friend suspiciously. Caron's talk about Way being a two-timer ... could she be yet another of the dead man's lovers? Was Caron getting drunk because she'd found out about Verdeaux and Aurora? Or because she was a lightweight?

'Can I have another cherry?' Caron asked Luc.

Lightweight.

Truth be told, I had seen an awful lot of fooling around in Brookhills. Some of it had involved Caron, which was why I was making a Brookhills into a mountin'.

I giggled and slapped a hand over my mouth. Apparently Caron wasn't the only one who couldn't hold her liquor. But then I had an excuse. I'd been assaulted. *And* pushed in the snow.

Jacque was talking to Luc. 'So how is it that you came to open your market in Benson Plaza?' he asked. 'I must admit that I worried when I established Schultz's, for fear our stores would compete for the same consumer.'

'And they didn't?' Sarah asked.

'Not really,' Luc said. 'People come to our store for meats, deli foods and breads and to Jacque's for fresh fish and seafood, specialty items.'

'Produce,' Jacque added. 'We pride ourselves on the freshest of produce.'

Which is one of the reasons the opening of Gross National Produce would be almost as much a disaster for Jacque, as it was for the rest of us.

Luc was answering Jacque's original question. 'Tien's mother, An, came here from Vietnam with me after the war. We lived with my folks for awhile and worked my ma's deli in Milwaukee. When Tien was born, my mother turned the business over to me and I moved it out here so Tien could grow up in the suburbs.'

'I was ... what, a year old when we came to Brookhills?' Tien said, looking adoringly at her father.

Luc nodded. 'Just before your mother died. It was very hard, but we – you and me – we kept it going.'

'At one year old,' Tien said, 'I must have been more of a burden than anything else.'

'Just having you around meant more to me than you'll ever know.' Luc picked up his drink, looked at it and set the glass back down on the counter. 'At any age.'

It was quiet for a moment, except for the icy snow pelting the windows outside.

'You've moved once,' Sarah said. 'You can do it again. I can find you a location that will be even better.'

Under other circumstances I would have put it down to a sales pitch. Somehow, now, I didn't believe that. Sarah was genuinely trying to help.

'No,' Luc said. 'I didn't like Way much, but he might have done us a favor. I can retire or go somewhere else and Tien can start a new life.'

'A new life?' Tien asked. 'Doing what?'

'You can go back to school,' Mrs G said,

trying to be optimistic. 'Or maybe you'll meet a nice boy.'

Tien just smiled. As a thirty-something, she probably figured the percentages were not in her favor.

'It's all Way's fault.' Caron had cut a wedge from the orange Tien had used to garnish the drinks and was dipping it in brandy. 'Him and this Naomi girl.' She pointed the knife at Verdeaux, punctuated by a crash of thunder.

Jacque took the knife away from her. 'You are half right.'

Not to mention half in the bag.

Jacque continued. 'I am not certain Way can be blamed. He was a man, after all.' He cocked his head toward Naomi Verdeaux. 'And my former wife has a way with men like Way. Ask Rudy.'

That was way too many 'ways' for me. As I opened my mouth to ask for clarification, I heard a sound.

Squish SLAP, squish SLAP, squish SLAP.

I glanced at the front door, expecting ... I'm not sure what I was expecting. Maybe *Mad Max: Beyond Thundersnow*? It couldn't be my attacker, after all. He, as Luc said, would be long gone. He sure wouldn't come knocking at the front door.

But no. Not only wasn't it Mad Max, but the sound wasn't coming from the front door, but rather the back. The service hallway. Uh-oh.

As one, we spun around on our lunch counter stools and regarded the door.

'Did anybody lock it?' I asked in my stage whisper.

'No,' Caron said breathlessly. Then she giggled.

Rudy stood up. 'It's probably Aurora.' He approached the door and I followed.

As Rudy reached the door, the noise stopped and the doorknob turned.

Probably wanting the advantage of surprise, Rudy pushed the door open. Preferring the advantage of cover, I hid behind him.

'Hey, watch out,' a familiar voice said.

'Bernie?' Caron called. She slipped off her stool and walked – a trifle unsteadily – to the door, then peeked over my shoulder into the dim hallway. 'Is that you?'

Bernie Egan, Caron's husband, had fallen ass over teakettle on to the concrete floor. His feet were waving in the air, one snowshoe on, the other nowhere in sight.

'How in the world did you get here?' Caron asked as she went to his aid.

'Umm, the snowshoes maybe?' I suggested as Rudy shook his head in disgust and went back to the rest of the group.

'But he just has one,' Caron pointed out.

Bernie sat up. 'Have you been drinking?'

'Nah,' she said. 'Eating fruit, mostly.'

Bernie looked at me.

'And maybe a little brandy,' I told him. 'Where's your other snowshoe?'

'At Uncommon Grounds. I couldn't get this one off, though.'

'I'll go get a knife,' Caron offered.

Having seen what she did to the orange, I didn't think that was such a good idea. 'Maybe I can get it undone.'

'I think a knife or scissors would be better,' Bernie said. 'I sort of jury-rigged it.'

I wasn't an expert on snowshoes, but it did look like it was held on by shoelaces and duct tape.

'Duct tape?' I asked, as I went back into the store for scissors.

'It's all I had.' Bernie, taking the scissors from me, slipped the blade between the duct tape and his boot. 'I have to admit, it held pretty well.'

I'd say. It was a good mile-and-a-half from Bernie and Caron's house to Benson Plaza.

He stood up. 'I couldn't get through to

Uncommon Grounds by telephone, so I got worried.' He put his hand on Caron's shoulder. 'I wanted to make sure she didn't try to drive.'

Especially under the influence of 'fruit'.

I was wondering how Bernie got into the coffee shop when he said, 'And Maggy, guess what? I have a surprise for you.'

For *me*?

A BMW perhaps? Or a nice bottle of red wine? I wasn't greedy. I was up for anything except, perhaps, another body.

Then in walked one.

FOURTEEN

'Eric!' I cried, instinctively going to throw both arms around my son who stands six inches taller than me. 'I'm so glad to see you.'

Then, because I *am* a mother, I pulled back and looked at him square on. 'What's wrong?'

His eyes dampened just a bit. Then, it was gone.

'Nothing's wrong,' he said with a smile. 'Can't a loving offspring just come visit?'

Not the week before final exams, he couldn't.

If I hadn't known better, I might have thought I'd imagined the look in Eric's eyes. But I knew better, because I knew my son.

He was projecting his hearty voice. The one he used around distant relatives and strangers he wanted to keep that way.

I nodded, willing to bide my time until he and I could talk in private about what was going on in his world. 'How did you get here?'

'Bernie,' Eric said, shrugging out of his pea coat. It wasn't warm enough for a snowstorm, but at least the kid had the sense to layer a sweatshirt under it.

'From Minneapolis? I think not.' I tipped up the hood to dump the accumulated snow and then reflexively looked around for Caron.

Happily, we were at Goddard's and Mrs G had a more positive puddle-posture than did my business partner.

'Eric, you poor boy,' our host said, not even bothering with the mini-mountain of snow I'd just dumped on her floor. 'You're soaking wet. Can I get you an egg salad sandwich?'

Eric, who was not into 'gooshy' things (as he termed all things soft when he was five), gave her a hug. 'Thanks, Mrs G, but I just ate.'

An outright lie, if I knew my son, though one designed to make Mrs G feel good and still get him off the hook. 'Do you have any chips left over, though?'

Mrs G gave him a cuff on the ear. 'That's not food,' she said and, of course, went off to get the potato chips.

I turned to Eric. 'Did you drive all the way

down in the snow?' I asked.

'There wasn't any from Minneapolis almost all the way to Delafield.'

Delafield was just west of us.

'By the time I pulled off the Interstate,' he continued, 'I couldn't believe my eyes. This much snow? In May?'

He was telling *me*.

'How did you know where I'd be?' I asked.

Eric gestured behind him. 'When I got home, Frank and you weren't there, so I figured that meant you'd be at the shop.' Even as he spoke, Frank came bounding up, followed by Oliver.

Oliver and Eric exchanged knuckle bumps and then settled down on either side of Frank. The sheepdog had dropped to the floor and flipped over on his back, the better to receive belly rubs.

Ahh. A boy and his dog. And another boy.

I turned to Bernie. 'So you found Eric in our parking lot?' I was still trying to piece together my son's trek.

'No, the corner of Brookhill and Poplar Creek. He slid off the road at the stop sign and landed in the ditch...' Bernie hesitated, like he didn't want it to look like he was tattling on Eric. 'The minivan is...'

I shook my head. 'I don't care what shape

my old Dodge Caravan is in, so long as Eric is safe.' And with me. I was still reveling in the fact that 'home' to my son was where Frank and I lived, rather than the Mc-Mansion his father occupied.

Petty, I know, but hey, I take my victories where I can find them. And today I found them on the wrong side of the proverbial tracks, in a tiny Brookhills house with blue stucco walls, a puke-green toilet and a gigantic, accident-prone sheepdog.

Life is good.

'Who else is here?' Bernie was asking. 'Is everyone safe?'

Caron took on the hostess role, albeit a bit unsteadily. 'I think you know everyone, Bernie: Luc, Tien, Rudy, Jacque, Sarah, Mrs Goddard, Oliver...'

As she spoke, I was hit by another pang of concern for Aurora, whom Caron hadn't mentioned. Out of sight, out of mind. But I also registered that with all the hubbub, I wasn't quite sure how long Aurora'd been gone. An hour maybe?

'Did you see anyone else coming in?' I asked Bernie. I was grateful to have Eric inside and safe. It would be nice if Aurora proved likewise.

'Not a soul,' Bernie said as he collapsed

into a booth. 'Don't be surprised, though. It's an ungodly mess out there.'

'The newsman says we have already the eighteen inches,' Jacque reported, holding up the yellow radio.

Bernie shook his head. 'That's in Milwaukee. Here in Brookhills, we're up to nearly two feet. It's the heavy stuff, but even so, the wind is causing drifts up to some rooflines. In order to get through, I had to snowshoe smack down the center of the road. Not that it mattered, because nothing is moving. In fact, the police are threatening to ticket people if they take their cars out.'

'Smart,' Luc said, nodding his head. 'A curfew'll keep everyone safe until they can clear the streets.'

'Not a fit night for man nor beast,' said Bernie. 'Or beasts, plural, I guess. I don't think even the animals can survive this. Believe it or not, Eric and I saw a pile of squirrels huddled together for warmth, right on Brookhill Road.'

I'd been looking out the window, trying to catch sight of Aurora. Now I turned. 'In the street?'

'Yeah,' Bernie said. 'Right in the middle of a snow drift at the corner. Damndest thing I've ever seen. I figured squirrels would hide in trees or maybe under things, like any other rodent.'

Bernie had it right. Squirrels usually stayed in their nests when it was cold and nasty. And their nests were in trees, not snow forts. 'Did these ... squirrels move?'

Bernie looked at me differently. 'Something wrong, Maggy?'

'It's just that Aurora went out some time ago to measure the snow and she hasn't come back.'

'*And,* she was wearing a squirrel coat,' Caron said as she drained Luc's glass, otherwise forgotten on the counter.

'Mink,' Verdeaux said irritably. 'It's sheared black mink. With a sable collar and cuffs.' She turned to me. 'You don't think...'

Bernie looked skeptical. 'These didn't look like mink. They were brown, with rings on them. Maybe I'm wrong about the squirrel part. Could be that it's a raccoon, I suppose. Even a whole family of them.'

I looked at Verdeaux.

'The sable trim has markings on it,' she admitted. 'I suppose it could look like...'

'I think we'd better check, don't you?' I looked around for my jacket, forgetting that it was soaking wet and still in Uncommon Grounds. The former, I could have put up with. The latter … well, there was no way I was going back there by myself.

Opting to dig through the tourist trash instead, I found a beach towel emblazoned with 'Milwaukee, a Great Place by a Great Lake' and wrapped it around myself.

Eric looked up. 'Nice fashion statement, Mom.'

Geez, everybody was a critic. Witness what *Project Runway* hath wrought.

Nonetheless, I looked down at my oversize T-shirt, tights and slipper-socks. 'You're right. Give me yours.'

Eric hoisted himself up off the floor and went across to the pea coat, which he'd slung over one of the stools at the lunch counter.

He lifted it. 'Wow. It's dripping.'

It was. A lot. 'That's all right. It still beats a beach towel.' Besides, my having Eric's jacket would prevent him from coming out with us, something I feared he, being curious and male, would want to do.

'Where are you going,' he asked. 'Can I go, too?'

'You don't have a coat,' I said sweetly, as I slipped his on. 'Bernie, can you show me where you saw the squirrels?'

As Bernie nodded, Luc stood up. 'You're not going out there alone, Maggy. I'll come with you.'

'No, I'll go,' Rudy and Jacque said in unison.

'Hey,' Bernie protested. 'I'm a guy and I'm going to be with her. It's not like she needs more protection, after all.'

Nobody met anyone's eyes.

'Right?' Bernie asked.

Still no answer.

Eric looked at me suspiciously. 'Mom?'

I cleared my throat. 'We, umm, we've had a...'

'My dad's dead.' Oliver gave Frank a final pat and stood up. 'Somebody killed him.'

Bernie looked from me to Caron and back again. 'Truly?'

The lawyer in him. I suppressed the urge to say, 'No, we just figured we'd tell the kid that.'

'No, we just figured we'd tell the kid that,' Sarah said.

It was like having my very own bad angel, one who didn't even need to sit on my left shoulder to say out loud what I was thinking.

'Mr Benson was killed?' This from Eric now. 'But how?'

'An accident with a snow-blower,' I said.

'And a hatchet,' Caron piped up. 'Don't forget that li'l detail.' She was picking her teeth with the business end of an umbrella-topped toothpick.

Bernie and Eric pivoted toward me, but Tien, surprisingly, was the one who took charge. 'Maggy found Way's body just as the storm was reaching its peak. We haven't been able to get in touch with the police, since, as you know –' she nodded toward Bernie – 'all the telephones are out.'

I said. 'Text message.'

Everyone looked at me.

'I was going to get my cellphone to see if I could text Eric, when I ... didn't...' I trailed off lamely. Eric and Bernie had just gotten there, after all, why pile on bad news?

I wasn't fooling Eric, though. 'Didn't *what*?' he demanded. God help me, but he had his mother's eyes and his father's im-patience.

'Oh, for Christ's sake.' Sarah had her own patience issues. 'The murderer knocked your mother down in making his getaway.'

I opened my mouth to protest, but that pretty much hit the nail of brevity on the head.

Eric gave me a dark look. 'You couldn't tell me that?'

'I didn't want you to worry,' I said and Eric's face changed.

'I get that,' he said.

He was letting me off the hook far too easily. Which meant he was not telling me something, so I wouldn't worry. Wasn't working.

'By the way,' he said, changing the subject. 'Text messaging isn't getting through either now. I tried it.'

He and I looked at each other. We needed to talk and both of us knew it.

Ducking that, Eric asked, 'So, umm, you think something might have happened to Mrs Benson?' He cocked his head toward Oliver.

'I'm sure she's fine,' I said. 'Maybe she even went for help, in fact.' Or had run into a homicidal maniac.

'And the "squirrels"?' This from Oliver.

'They're probably just that,' Tien said, stepping in. She was closest to Oliver and Eric's age, and therefore had more standing in their eyes. 'But we'll never know until we look. If your mother did fall down or some-thing –' she'd engaged Oliver now – 'she might need help.'

If it *was* Aurora out there, I was afraid she was beyond help.

'Besides,' Tien continued, rubbing her arms, 'maybe we can find something to burn. The fire in the wood stove is almost out.'

'Whoever wants to come, you're welcome,' I said, though I didn't see the attraction of sloshing through the snow toward what might very well be a dead body. In fact, if they all wanted to go I'd be happy to stay inside and tend the stove.

Nah, who was I kidding? I had every intention of seeing for myself.

In the end, we left Caron to finish off the dregs of everyone else's brandy old-fashioneds. Mrs G, Eric and Oliver were staying as well, though the last two, not happily.

Eric insisted I take Frank 'for protection'. I started to argue, but our sheepdog had been staunch when I'd been attacked. I actually wanted him with me.

I also wanted him to pee outside for once.

We trooped through the door and out into the storm, Bernie leading the way with a Scooby Doo Flashlight ($9.99), me on his heels and Frank on mine. Bernie had insisted that I wear his rabbit fur hat. I pulled down my earflaps.

'You look like Rocky the Flying Squirrel,' Sarah said, catching up to me.

Of Rocky and Bullwinkle – the old, but – back then – cutting-edge cartoon show. I remembered Rocky wearing one of those antique aviator caps. I thought his cap was leather, but given that Rocky was furry, himself, I guessed it all balanced out.

'At least my head is warm.' I swore that when I got home, I was going to sink into a hot bathtub and never come out. Frank would lie on the bathmat next to me and bring me whatever I needed. 'Do your business, Frank,' I urged as we cleared the front sidewalk.

Sarah looked sideways at me. 'We're stuck here in this nightmare of a storm, with one person murdered and another likely at the business end of a snowdrift. And you're worrying about your *dog*?'

'He's got a bladder the size of Lake Michigan,' I said, pausing to let Frank sniff around. 'Believe this, you don't want to be close when he lets loose.'

Ignoring the warning, Sarah leaned down to snarl in my ear, but all she got was a noseful of rabbit fur. 'Focus, dammit,' she said, rubbing her tickling nose. 'People might be dropping like flies.'

'I get that. But it's not like there's something I can do about it. We're stuck here.'

'Then stop finding bodies, dammit.'

As Sarah spoke, Frank let loose. I believe

it's called the fire hose effect. She couldn't say I didn't warn her.

Knowing that the two of them were up to the challenge, I left Frank to Sarah's tender mercies and, as the rest of the group hung back, approached the pile of snow on Brookhill Road. Just as Bernie had said, it did look like a family of squirrels or raccoons had made their nest there. I signaled Verdeaux to come closer. 'Don't trample the area, but can you see? Is that your coat?'

'I can't tell,' she said irritably. Verdeaux stepped in a little more and peered at the dark-colored tangle. It had begun snowing harder again, making it tough to tell if the mass was black or brown. 'For all we know it's the big brother of that stupid hat you have on.'

Yeah, yeah, yeah. I took one more step and leaned down. Holding my breath, I reached out and touched the material. It was fur. However, I couldn't tell what it was attached to. I tangled my fingers in the fur to get a grip and pulled up. The material came away easily.

A hood. Fur-trimmed.

And beneath it, Aurora Benson's blonde head, streaked here and splotched there with blood.

FIFTEEN

'Now I'm sorry I called her the Weather Slut,' Sarah said to me.

We were crouched down next to Aurora's body. Any hope of keeping the crime scene intact was lost when Naomi Verdeaux started to scream and Frank came running.

I was of the opinion that Verdeaux was more distraught about the blood on her coat than she was about Aurora's death. But then I'm a cynic.

Frank, on the other hand, didn't care why Verdeaux was screaming. He just wanted part of the action.

'I think Aurora kind of liked the slut thing,' I said. 'Especially as she ... well, aged out.'

Sarah nodded. 'Like old ladies don't mind being called girls.'

Personally, I've never minded being called a girl. Sure beats other things I'd been called.

'Yes, like that.' Gently, I brushed the snow

off Aurora's back. 'Well, that's a relief, at least.'

'What?'

'No cleaver.'

'Unless the murderer used it on the back of her head.' Even Sarah, as tough a broad as she was – or tried to act – seemed shocked.

'I don't think there's enough blood for that kind of wound,' I said, going for observant, yet detached. It was either play professional or run back to Goddard's and hide under a counter. Or maybe throw up. Egg salad and bloodied bodies – especially that of someone who might have become a friend – don't mix.

'Maybe she wouldn't bleed as much with the cold and snow,' Sarah suggested, presumably following my lead. 'You know ... umm ... coagulation?'

We looked at the matted mess in Aurora's hair.

'There is that,' I said.

'Bring her inside.' A voice from above.

I pivoted and looked up. The speaker was Rudy.

I shook my head. 'No way. Pavlik will have our heads if we move either of the bodies.'

Even as I said it, I realized how ridiculous my reply sounded.

Especially after I'd done such a great job 'preserving the scenes'. In back, the snow around Way's body had been trampled by all of us, not to mention by Frank and my attacker. *Then* it had been covered by fresh snow.

The same thing would happen to Aurora's body, I thought, as Frank raced around us in ever widening circles, barking excitedly and spraying snow as he went.

Rudy put his hands out, palms up. 'What do you want to do? Leave her here for the plows?'

A good point. The trucks – garbage haulers during the warm months, with snow blades attached for the winter – would come out as soon as the plows were readied and the storm tapered off. We couldn't very well post someone outside overnight to ward them off when they arrived.

'I guess we could put her in back,' I said.

'Next to Way?' Verdeaux, who was still eyeing her coat, asked. 'She'd probably like that.'

I'd prefer to plant Verdeaux next to Way. Permanently.

Before I could say anything snotty, Luc intervened. 'Listen, I was thinking about that. I hate to say it, but we have predators and scavengers out here. Coyotes, crows, hawks. And they're probably getting pretty hungry by now.'

Ugh. In the space of a few hours, I'd gone from serving lattes in an upscale suburban coffee house to a walk-on role in *Wild Kingdom*.

'Maybe we should bring them both inside,' Luc said, waiting for Frank to pass by on his circuit before he joined us.

'Bodies stink,' I said with the certainty of personal experience.

Rudy, who, like Luc, had been in the Vietnam War, apparently had the same kind of experience. 'Even with the hallways as cold as they are, corpses will thaw and then decompose pretty quickly.'

'We can put them in my freezer,' Luc offered. 'It's almost empty and, even with the electricity out, they'll probably stay frozen.'

Corpse-sicles.

'You want two bodies in your deli?' I asked.

Luc shrugged. 'It's not mine any more. And if Gross National Produce wants to keep the fixtures for some reason, they'll just have to get things cleaned.'

Worked for me, assuming Gross's customer base could get over the eventual news stories that would describe the freezer's most recent contents in the kind of detail usually reserved for a celebrity's fall from grace.

We sent the rest of the group back to Goddard's and, with Rudy and Luc doing the heavy lifting, managed to get Aurora's body out of the street and to the front door of Luc's store. From there, God help us, we put her in a shopping cart and wheeled her into the freezer. Then we took a second cart through the service hallway to get Way.

'Pavlik is going to kill me,' I moaned, as we surveyed the walk-in freezer after we were done. There was no emergency lighting inside, of course, so I'd run to the store and gotten one of the paper lanterns ($7.99). It added a bizarrely festive air to the scene.

Aurora was still in her cart, but Way was stiff enough that we had needed to balance him diagonally from the handle to the nose of the cart in order to traverse the narrow hallway to An's. Once we got his body to the freezer, we lifted him off and took Way in, feet first. He was lying face down on a shelf next to the frozen peas, cleaver and all.

I shuddered.

'Let's get you out of here, Maggy.'

Luc was eyeing my tights-clad legs, not in a *God-but-you're-hot* kind of manner, but more of a *God-you-look-cold-and-stupid* one.

'With how you're dressed, you're going to catch pneumonia.'

'I'll just be happy if I don't catch a meat cleaver in the back,' I said to him. Then I lowered my voice and gestured Luc to move away from Rudy, who was backing the cart out of the cooler. 'That cleaver in Way's back. Do you recognize it?'

'How could I recognize a—'

'I mean, is it one of yours?'

'It might be, Maggy, but those things are pretty standard,' Rudy interjected before Luc could answer. The man must have the radar of a bat. 'Besides Luc and Tien sold off their stock. Anyone could have one.'

That was true, I guessed. Even I had a cleaver at home that looked similar. I used it to cut pizza. And pretty much everything else. Except people. I draw the line at people.

Luc looked surprised that Rudy was defending him. 'I had three or four cleavers – all slightly different sizes and shapes. It's hard to tell whether this is one of them without pulling it out.'

'We *sure* aren't doing *that*,' I said flatly, closing the freezer door, 'even if it were possible.' I remembered trying to pick up the 'shovel'. The blade was either frozen in or stuck deep into bone. Or both.

I shuddered again. 'Luc, were all the cleavers sold?' I'm not Pavlik, my method of interrogation being more oblique. You've heard of Good Cop, Bad Cop? I'd be more Wimpy Cop.

And, the Wimp Method seldom got immediate results.

Now Luc shrugged. 'So far as I know. Tien might have a better idea. She took everything we didn't sell over to Goodwill.'

'Are you thinking a cleaver killed Aurora, too?' Rudy slid the cart we'd used to transport Way's body into the line of stacked ones by the door.

Luc cringed and pulled our 'hearse' back out again, rolling it into the corner, where it couldn't interact with – and infect – its cousins.

'If so,' Rudy continued, not seeming to notice, 'that means there are at least two.'

At *least* two? Like he was entertaining the possibility there might be a third cleaver with somebody else's name on it?

I said, 'We'll probably have to wait until the professionals get here to figure out what killed Aurora.' A thought struck me. 'If it was something sharp like a cleaver or an axe, though, it should have cut the hood of the coat.'

'Could you tell through the fur?' Luc asked.

'I don't know,' I admitted. 'Maybe by looking at the inside of the hood, but it's probably lined with fur, too. I was so shook by finding her that I didn't think to look.'

'Understandable,' Rudy said, opening up the door to the hall and ushering us out. 'Why don't you and Luc go back to Goddard's and get warm? I'm going to my barbershop to see if I can find anything we can burn in Gloria's wood stove. Whatever we could dig up outside would be too wet to burn, anyway.'

We separated in the back hallway, Rudy turning toward his shop, Luc and I heading in the opposite direction toward Goddard's. The pharmacy was somber as the two of us entered.

Sarah and Mrs Goddard were with Oliver. A year ago, I would have said Sarah was the last person I'd want trying to give support to a boy who had lost both parents in the space of a few hours. But I knew first-hand that I'd been wrong about that.

When Patricia Harper, Sarah's good friend – and Caron's and my partner in Uncommon Grounds – had been killed the morning

the store opened, Sarah had taken in Sam
and Courtney, Patricia's children. The real-
estate broker had turned out to be just what
they needed. And vice versa. In fact, the last
phone call that actually connected from Uncommon Grounds had been Sarah's to her
two teenaged charges, making sure they were
both home and safe.

Now she and Mrs G were sitting with
Oliver by the dwindling fire of the wood
stove, each in a beach chair with an umbrella
over it.

'So, do you think you'll sell the mall?'
Sarah was asking Oliver. 'I can probably get
you a good price for the property.'

'Sarah, for God's sake,' I said, grabbing her
shoulder. 'Please tell me you're not hustling
business from a seventeen-year-old, who's
been orphaned within the last twenty-four
hours.'

'Hey.' She pried my fingers off her arm.
'Oliver asked me.'

'He's probably in shock.' Or, perhaps,
coolly assessing his inheritance?

'No.' Sarah rubbed her palms on the thighs
of her slacks. 'Oliver is a young adult with no
visible means of support. His parents are
dead and he doesn't know where his next
pair of jeans is coming from.' Sarah rose and

walked over to the lunch counter.

'Mrs Thorsen, I don't want to sell Benson Plaza,' Oliver said, angling the chair's umbrella so he could see me. 'On the other hand, though, I know it takes money to keep things going. Thing is –' he shrugged helplessly, and I realized he had tears in his eyes – 'I just don't have any.'

I sat down in the chair Sarah had vacated. It was good to be close to the fire so my clothes could dry, but that wasn't my main purpose. 'You don't have to worry about that right now, Oliver.'

'But he does,' Mrs G said. 'When Hank died, I had to think about all sorts of problems. Taxes, insurance, even the money for burying him. People kept saying don't worry about it, but they were wrong. Dead wrong.'

'I'm sure it's been tough.' I didn't know if she would tell me about the foreclosure on their home, but I figured I'd give her the opportunity if she wanted to take it.

She didn't. 'I'm doing just fine now,' she said, patting Oliver on the hand. 'It's Oliver I want to make sure is protected. Right?'

She looked at Oliver. 'Right?' she repeated, still without receiving any answer.

'He's asleep,' I said.

I was trying to remember if it was the

guilty or the innocent who were able to fall asleep in their cells.

It was supposed to be a 'tell', like something an opponent does during a poker game that tips you to the fact they're bluffing. Tapping their cards. Rubbing their eyes.

Or, in my case, sweating bullets.

I sighed and looked around for Eric. The store was quiet, everybody unusually subdued. Or maybe they were just afraid to talk to the wrong person and, thereby, end up dead.

Beyond that, though, the air was getting colder and the lights were growing noticeably dimmer. The generator must be running on fumes. Even our battery-powered Japanese lanterns seemed to be waning.

In the lessening light, I saw figures ransacking shelves two aisles over. I started to excuse myself to see what they were doing and then realized Mrs G was asleep, too.

Sarah, on the other hand, was already up from her stool at the lunch counter and heading for 'Seasonal Items' in the corner of Goddard's.

'They're like locusts,' she said surveying the swarm as we turned the corner. 'They've taken everything.'

The shelves were indeed empty, but I

couldn't imagine what had been on them that anybody would want to seize. 'Took what?'

'Lawn chairs, of course, though Gloria, Oliver and I got the best ones, thank God. Still, I really wanted a tablecloth. Aha!' She pulled out a folded square of red and white checked plastic that had been shoved in the back of the bottom shelf. 'Got one!'she said, waving the package triumphantly.

I looked at her.

She looked at me. 'I mean, unless you need it.'

'Enjoy your bounty, however unexpected,' I said, shaking my head. 'Just consider the "flannel no-slip backing" a gift from me.'

I looked around at where people had 'set-up camp' – some in pairs and others alone, but all protecting their turf.

But no sign of my son. I was getting worried.

'Have you seen Eric?' I asked Sarah.

'He was heading to the men's room with a magazine as I came in,' Sarah said distractedly. 'Moving fast, so I thought it best not to stand in his way.'

Good thinking. Eric took after his father that way. One did not disturb the Thorsen men and their reading in the bathroom. If I'd known how educational the location was, I would have sent Eric there instead of summer school when he fell behind in second-grade reading.

Though how in the world could anybody stay in the mall bathroom for any length of time, given the lack of water for flushing or washing?

'I handed him a pine-tree air freshener to hang in there,' Sarah said, as if, yet again, she'd read my mind. Now about ten feet down the aisle, she was letting some of the air out of a beach ball that looked like a yellow cat's eye marble.

'Pillow?' I guessed.

'Shh,' she said, her finger to her lips. 'Everybody will want one.'

They could have mine. I looked around.

Caron and Bernie's little piece of paradise was in the cosmetics aisle. Naomi Verdeaux had made herself comfortable in a private room – the photo department. The smell of rotten eggs emanating from the vats could have been caused by the film-processing chemicals, or maybe the egg salad was making an unfortunate encore performance. Either way, I thought Verdeaux could be fairly certain no one would breach her walls voluntarily.

Just to be sure, though, Jacque stood guard at the photo check-out counter, examining photos by fading lantern. Tien and Luc were tending the stove, feeding it brown grocery bags from their store and ancient, tattered magazines from Rudy's shop.

Meanwhile, the barber wandered the male enhancement aisle.

'*Lord of the Flies* transplanted to a strip mall,' I muttered to Sarah.

She looked at me quizzically. 'The movie where the plane crashes and the kids have to fend for themselves?'

'Kind of,' I said, 'but you're talking about the second screen adaption of the original cult novel by William Golding. In the book, itself, it's British school kids shipwrecked on an island.'

'Ohhhh, you mean the one where the boys, believing the rest of the world has been destroyed by the atom bomb, despair of rescue and create their own micro-society in which there are two factions, one civilized and one savage, who battle each other with tragic results?'

'Umm, yeah,' I said. 'That would be the one.'

Sarah shrugged. 'I'm not sure that egg salad and Caron filching drinks quite cuts it,' she said, reclaiming the chaise longue I'd vacated. She covered herself with the table-cloth she'd appropriated and gave me the thumbs-up before settling back on the beach ball pillow. 'If anybody butchers a pig, though, be sure to let me know.' Her eyes closed.

I was still trying to get over a deflation worse than even the beach ball had suffered at my friend's hands, when Eric stuck his head in the door.

'Want to talk?' I asked him softly.

He looked uncomfortable. 'Not now, Mom. I mean, with everybody...'

I held up my finger to indicate Eric should wait and I returned to the photo counter. Naomi Verdeaux had let herself into Way's office. That meant she had a key.

Jacque was gone from his post at the counter, but his ex-wife was perched on the photo technician's stool, her head on the big film-processing machine's keyboard. I'd have worried that she was going to break the thing if I didn't know it hadn't worked in years. I'd also be worried the wheeled stool was going to slide right out from under Verdeaux, but ... I honestly didn't give a damn.

The sign at the counter said 'Ring for

service' so I tapped the reception-style bell lightly to get Verdeaux's attention. No response, so I smacked it a little harder, only to be rewarded by choruses of 'hey!' and 'quiet!' from every corner of the pharmacy save the photo area. So much for service.

I walked around the end of the counter and tapped Verdeaux, instead of the bell.

But, still, ominously, no sign of life.

SIXTEEN

Please, God, I thought, please don't tell me I've stumbled on another body.

I considered walking away. Let somebody else 'discover' this one. Later.

I mean, I said to myself, it already smells bad in here. Who would notice?

The corpse opened one eye. 'Go … a … way,' Verdeaux said stiffly. Succinctly, too.

'I need the key to Way's office.'

'Too bad.' The eye closed again.

I was in no mood to play Odysseus to the other woman's Cyclops. Though I'd have dearly loved to shove a pickle spear through her eye.

I shook Verdeaux by the shoulder. 'The key,' I demanded.

She growled and shifted slightly, causing the stool to roll. I blocked its progress with my foot. 'Again, the key.'

She propped her head on one hand and eyed me. 'The door's open.'

That seemed un-Way-like. 'Do you mean you left it unlocked?'

The growl looked to become a snarl. I let my foot slide and Verdeaux went with it.

Naomi grabbed either side of the desk to keep herself from falling. 'Damn it, *what* is your problem?'

I wanted to say, '*You* are my problem,' like we were squabbling twelve-year-olds. Instead, I decided to rise above such.

'You,' I said. 'You're my problem.'

That'd show her. 'Now tell me,' I continued, 'which door is open, the outside one or the back one? Because if you left it unlocked, I want the key so I can secure it. There's a murderer running around and I'd prefer not to give him unfettered private access, you know?'

I also preferred not to walk into Way's office with Eric, without knowing if my intruder had circled the mall and come back in that entrance.

I looked toward my son, who was staring at the floor. Something was really wrong. Was Eric sick? Flunking out? Or was he thrown out? Maybe in the context of trouble with the law?

All the bad things that could happen to my nineteen-year-old son, all the ways a young life could be ended or changed forever, were racing through my head.

Oh, my God: was I going to be a grandma?

'Now!' I screamed at Verdeaux. 'I need to have the key now!'

Every sleepy visage in the place popped up over its respective store shelf. When each saw who I was brow-beating, though, they stuck their little turtle-heads back into their shells.

Verdeaux, probably assuming I was a psycho, also must have sensed a decided lack of support from her fellow travelers. As a result, she became more forthcoming.

'The back door, damn it. What do you think I did, go outside in this crap?' She gestured toward the window, the growl now a defensive snarl. 'The door from the service hallway was sitting open so I went in.'

'It was open?' As I've said, it wasn't like Way to leave either of his office doors open. God forbid we should be able to share and compare leases or something.

'Open. Ajar. Whatever you want to call it. I never had a key. And I sure as hell don't have one now.'

Oh.

'Well, thanks,' I said.

I walked back to the rear door, thinking. If the hallway one was open, maybe something had happened to make Way leave it that way. Could he have been forced to retrieve something from his office before he was killed?

But that made no sense. Why would the killer have Way don a coat and start up the snow-blower before killing him? Wouldn't it have been easier to murder Way in his office without a winter coat to slice through? By the time anyone found our landlord's body, the bad guy could be long gone.

'Let's go to Way's office,' I said to Eric, as I commandeered a lemon-yellow lantern. 'We can talk there.'

He just nodded and followed me down the hall. Sure enough, the door was still open. Leave it to Verdeaux not to close the door after herself.

I made Eric wait and stepped in cautiously, holding the lantern out in front of me to illuminate the space. Assuming the outside doors were all locked, there would be no way for my attacker to get back into the mall and the office should be safe. That was a big assumption, though.

I held the lantern out and swung it around slowly, illuminating the office section by section. Way's mahogany desk and matching leather chair. The two pieces were much too big for the space, but given the gigantic fireplace that took up one entire wall of my blue stucco living room and my super-sized sheepdog, I had a bit of a glasshouse problem there.

The only other furniture in the office was a bank of file cabinets along one wall and a reception desk piled high with newspapers. Oh, and a leatherette visitors' couch. I hated to think what kind of action the thing had hosted.

'If these walls could talk,' I said under my breath as I moved aside to let Eric in.

'Do they have walls that do that now?' he asked, looking at me with new-found appreciation. 'Did you see those mirrors that turn into flat-screen televisions?'

Eric is so far ahead of me, technologically speaking, that I've given up even trying to keep up.

'Cool,' I said, which should give you an idea of which millennium I'm still stuck in.

Before I could stop him, Eric sank on to the couch, which had probably seen more traffic than the street outside. Ah, well. Way probably had a cleaning service.

I sat down next to Eric.

He looked at me.

I looked at him.

All the awful things started going through

my head again. Early grandparenthood was starting to look mighty good.

'Give,' I said, after a moment.

Eric's eyes filled with tears.

With a rush, I put my arm around his shoulder. He laid his head on my shoulder. Then he started to sob.

I rubbed his back and repeated all those things I crooned to him when he was nineteen months, not nineteen years, old. And every time he was sick or hurt. Every time I hugged him, every time I bandaged an elbow or made macaroni and cheese – they all came roaring back.

'Whatever it is,' I whispered in his ear, 'we'll take care of it together. You and me. No matter what.'

He pulled away and closed his eyes. Then he took a deep breath.

'Mom, I'm gay.'

SEVENTEEN

'Oh, thank God!' I practically passed out with relief.

'You mean it's OK with you?' Eric asked, his face a mix of relief and disbelief.

'*OK* with me? This is about you, not me. And whatever you do, so long as you act responsibly and stay safe, is OK with me.'

I put my hands on his shoulders and forced him to meet my eyes. '*You* are "OK" with me.'

He looked away. 'Dad told me it'll kill Grandma Thorsen.'

My first thought was, Eric told Ted before me?

My second thought: The old bat's eighty, if she's a day. Besides, she's had a good life.

Nevertheless, I told Eric, 'Grandma is tougher than Dad thinks.' I took a deep breath. 'And I have a feeling her reaction will be the same as mine.'

And if not, she'll go quickly and Eric won't

173

hear the details.

'If Dad ever tells her,' Eric said, with a little laugh. A very little laugh, but it was the first 'old Eric' I'd seen since he'd arrived at the mall.

'God, Eric.' I pulled him toward me. 'I thought you were going to tell me you were dying. Or maybe failing.'

A full-out laugh now. 'You'd rather I be gay than flunking out?'

I thought about it. 'Yeah. Yeah, I guess – no, I'm sure I would.'

We both laughed.

I held my son, each of us quiet for a moment. 'You know that this isn't the easiest path, right?' I asked him finally. 'Even these days?'

He nodded his head. 'I know. But it's the only ... path for me.'

I got that. 'How long ... I mean, when did you know that...' I realized I was making a mess of this.

Luckily, Eric saved me from myself. 'I'm not sure, honestly. I guess it just always ... was.'

I got that, too. I also got that there had been a whole lot of 'ellipsis-ing' going on between us. Not that we were leaving things unsaid, so much as that we were saying them carefully.

But this wasn't the time or the place for twenty questions. Except for one, maybe. 'You're being safe?'

'I'm not an idiot, Mom,' Eric said, and in that moment we were back to our normal relationship. Nagging mother, teenaged son.

'Yeah, yeah, yeah.' I matched his tone. 'So when are you going back to school? Exams next week, you know.'

'Have you noticed it's snowing?' Eric pointed out the window. 'Who knows when I can *get* back?'

'It's Thursday,' I said, standing up. 'It'll melt tomorrow and you can drive back this weekend.'

A sudden thought struck me. 'Is there something else you haven't told me?' I asked. 'You drove all the way down here. Was it just to tell—'

'That's it,' Eric said, and then he turned sheepish. 'The thing is that I told Dad over the phone and it didn't go all that well. After that disaster, I thought I'd better see you in person.'

'Why did you tell Dad?' I asked, trying not to sound whiny. Or petty. Or immature. It was a tough bill to fill, since I was all three.

'Before you, you mean?'

I'd heard there comes a time when the child becomes the parent, and the parent becomes the child. I just didn't know it was going to be so soon. 'OK, yes. Before me.'

Eric shrugged. 'Stupid, I guess.'

'I guess.' The two of us laughed and stood up. 'Should we go back to Goddard's?'

Eric pointed to the newspapers on the reception desk. 'Should we take those for the fire?'

Since Way was dead, and I'd never seen a receptionist occupying the desk, I doubted anyone would miss the papers.

'Why not?' I said, gesturing to Eric to grab the top half of the stack.

As Eric complied, I eyed the desk.

'Don't get any ideas,' he warned, sliding the papers under his arm. 'We'd need an axe to chop it apart.'

I sincerely hoped there wasn't an axe around. A meat cleaver was bad enough.

I went to pick up the rest of the newspapers and stopped.

'What?' Eric asked, already at the door.

I was still looking at the desk. 'This drawer,' I said. 'It looks broken.'

'So what?' Relieved of the burden of his secret, Eric seemed his old self again. 'You figure it will burn?'

I shook my head, and pointed to the splintered wood poking out of the top of the drawer. 'It looks like somebody forced the lock.'

'You think someone broke in?'

I slid out the drawer. 'If they did, they took anything worthwhile. Nothing but an old phonebook left.'

Eric was looking around. 'Mr Benson's desk drawers are open, too. And the file cabinet.'

He was right. While a couple of the drawers were closed tight, one had papers hanging out. The remainder were open an inch or two. Just the top drawer, the only one with a key lock, had been forced.

By whom?

Naomi Verdeaux had been in Way's office earlier to 'use the bathroom'. Had she been looking for something? And if so, what?

And, perhaps most importantly, had she found it?

EIGHTEEN

When we re-entered Goddard's, things were much as they had been. Mostly cold and mostly dark, with puddles of neon colors from lanterns hung here and there. The thunder was still sounding overhead and the snow was still coming down outside the window.

Even as things change, they stay the same. My son is gay.

The reaction I'd had when he told me was genuine. But another feeling was starting to creep in, too. Guilt. How long had he been carrying around this secret, worried that the people he loved most would stop loving him because of it? And why didn't I sense his fear? Why couldn't I have helped him?

'Help me stoke the fire,' Eric said, with the enthusiasm for fire-making of every guy I've ever met.

'You got it,' I said, following him over to the wood stove with my stack of newspapers.

Mrs G, Sarah and Oliver were still asleep on the lounge chairs.

I opened the door of the stove and Eric started crumpling individual sheets of newspaper. Then he rolled maybe six pages worth into a baton, bent the result in half and tied it into a tight knot at the center.

'Why are you doing that?'

'The sheets alone burn too fast, Mom, and just stuffing whole paper in the stove won't let them burn at all. This way –' he pointed to the flared corners at either end – 'the edges catch like kindling and the knot acts like a little log, or maybe a brick of charcoal.'

'Great.' I was amazed, both at the process and the fact that Eric, a child of the backyard gas grill era, knew what charcoal was. 'Where did you learn all this?'

'Boy Scouts.'

'Of course,' I said, remembering. 'You got a merit badge for camping, didn't you? I found a whole bunch of those patches in the kitchen drawer the other day.'

Eric looked at me. 'You know you were supposed to sew them on to my Boy Scout tunic, right?'

'Sew?'

'Whatssup?' Sarah's voice interrupted from under her coveted tablecloth.

'We're just stoking the fire,' I said, happy to have Eric diverted. If God wanted merit badges on shirts, he would have made them iron-on.

'You find Eric?' my friend asked, groggily. 'He OK?'

'He's great,' I assured her, as Eric poked the fire with a yardstick. 'Go back to sleep.'

'Okey-dokeeey.' The last syllable morphed into a snorty snore.

'Sarah can sleep anywhere,' Eric observed.

'You should talk. Remember that photo of you when we came back from the fair? You couldn't have been more than four. You were so exhausted that you fell asleep with your legs in the hallway and your head, one step down in the living room.

'Like Frank sleeps now.' Eric grinned.

'But not as furry.' I touched my son's arm. 'I think you should try to get some sleep.'

'I think I want to tend the stove for a while,' he said. 'You try, though.'

I agreed and, leaving him playing happily with fire, returned to the party aisle to scavenge.

As I feared, all the really good stuff was gone. Picking through the party favors, I came up with a flashlight that looked like a miniature rip-off of the Star Wars light saber (2 for $4.99) and Sponge Bob tablecloths ($7.69 each), but only paper, no flannel lining.

Which wouldn't be such a big deal if somebody hadn't appropriated my Milwaukee beach towel.

Sponge Bob would have to do. I thought about getting Eric one, too, but since it was paper, I figured he'd just burn it anyway.

I shook out the tablecloth and Sponge Bob stared back at me. I looked around for a quiet place for us to settle down and think.

And where better than the aisle I was in? Stripped of everything anybody could want, and it had only one way in and out. I sat down on the linoleum floor at the end of the aisle, my back against the stationery display. I'd be facing toward anybody approaching and I could keep an eye on Eric beyond the end of the aisle at the wood stove.

When Way was killed, I was content to keep a low profile. I didn't even want to think about who had taken his life, because ... well, frankly, I didn't really care much. Besides, the murderer was likely somebody I *did* like, and I didn't want to be in the position of pointing fingers.

Again.

But then I'd been attacked in the hallway and now Aurora was dead, too, leaving me with two more questions: who was the Bensons' killer, and why?

The most tempting suspect would be a stranger – the man in the hallway. But it didn't feel right to me. Why would he kill Way and Aurora in separate locations and by different methods, but spare me?

Yes, maybe Frank had saved me, but now that I'd had some relatively stress-free time to think about it, it seemed that Luc was right. The guy had just been trying to get away, making me more of a hindrance than a target.

But get away from what?

If my attacker was also Way's killer, why would he hang around outside in the snow, lying in wait to ambush Aurora hours later? It couldn't be a coincidence. Way and Aurora were ex-spouses and business partners. I didn't think this was just some madman, killing people in an unexpected storm. It didn't make sense.

On the other hand, what if all this violence was directly related to Benson Plaza? After all, both victims had been Bensons, leaving only one member of the family alive.

Did that put Oliver Benson in danger, too?

I looked down the aisle to where the poor kid was sleeping, safe for now. Eric was still sitting cross-legged on the floor, watching the fire, and Frank, who had been nosing around the store most of the night, had settled in next to him.

Eric was nineteen. An adult, legally. Oliver was two years younger and now alone.

Who would Oliver tell if he were gay? Or had just aced a test, or gotten a new job?

I tried to stop the thought fragments spinning through my head like lemons in an old slot machine.

All right. Assuming it was an inside job, Naomi Verdeaux was my top choice as suspect. First of all, I didn't like her. Secondly, she'd been in Way's office and had been uncooperative when I'd asked her for the key to its door.

Verdeaux also hadn't mentioned the break-in to me or anyone else, so far as I knew. It was possible she hadn't noticed if, indeed, the woman had gone in there only to use the bathroom. After all, Eric and I had been in the office for quite a while before we noticed the disarray.

As for motive, Aurora had threatened to back out of the Gross National Produce project. That certainly would have ticked

Verdeaux off. So maybe she decided to search the office, looking for documents that would tell her just how far Aurora had gone to stymie the plans.

Then, finding none, Verdeaux had killed Aurora before the surviving co-owner of Benson Plaza could do anything official to prevent Gross National Produce from moving in.

Or, Verdeaux found what she was looking for, destroyed whatever it was – maybe even in the wood stove – and then killed Aurora so no one would be the wiser.

But even if Naomi Verdeaux had killed Aurora, why kill Way?

I thought about that.

Despite her denial, maybe Verdeaux *had* discovered that Way was back with Aurora and wasn't as nonchalant about the relationship as she pretended. She might not be sentimental, but Verdeaux sure as hell was competitive. If she believed Aurora had usurped her side of Way's bed and then Way had betrayed her professionally, she might be capable of murder.

Capable, perhaps, but I didn't see her as a woman who would sacrifice business for pleasure. And from a purely financial point of view, killing Way and Aurora would accomplish less than nothing. It could only mean that Oliver would inherit and likely keep the mall as-is.

Unless she planned on romancing the seventeen-year-old boy she'd just orphaned, too.

Ugh.

Hell, I didn't know what *I* was thinking half the time, how could I know what was in other people's heads?

So if motive wasn't getting me anywhere, maybe opportunity might prove more advancing. Two murders, plenty of people around. If I could figure out where everyone was when each crime was committed, I might find that one of us was nearby – but not accounted for – when both Way and Aurora were killed.

Pushing Sponge Bob aside, I stood up and commandeered an eight-pack of 'Hi! My name is...' name badges and a Hannah Montana pen. I didn't check the prices first. This was, after all, an emergency.

Settling back down, I wrote names and whereabouts on each badge and laid them out on the worn linoleum floor. It took four more packs of badges – these plain, the better to have writing space – but I finally finished and sat back to survey my work.

Hi! My Name is Suspects	Hi! My Name is Way's Death	Hi! My Name is Aurora's Death
Caron Egan	With Maggy in UG	With Maggy in Goddard's
Aurora Benson	Had just left UG in search of Way	Dead
Naomi Verdeaux	Arrived at UG just after snow-blower goes silent	In Way's restroom, supposedly, then at Goddard's
Jacque Oui	Goddard's? Had just left UG	In Goddard's
Oliver Benson	?	Making egg salad with Mrs G
Mrs G	In UG	Making egg salad with Oliver
Rudy Fischer	In UG when snow-blower stops	Getting brandy old-fashioned mixings
Luc Romano	?	Gone to get more drink mixers
Tien Romano	?	In Goddard's
Bernie Egan	Home	On his way to Goddard's – found Eric, saw body

I reviewed the list for maybe a count of ten before cuffing myself in the head. Of course:

Big help, since his identity, whereabouts and motives were all a mystery. Still, it would be remiss of me not to list him.

I hunkered over the array of badges, which took up the full width of the aisle and ran the length of the greeting cards, from the close-out 'Happy Easter' cards to the timeless 'Congratulations on your Batmizvah'.

I could rule out Caron – and not just because she was my friend. God knows that hadn't stopped me from putting her on different suspect lists before. Fact was, though, we'd been together for both murders. First, when the snow-blower was stopped, apparently by Way's head, and later, when Aurora was killed. That was good enough for me.

Way and Aurora were in the clear, too. Not that it did them much good, what with being dead and all.

Bernie couldn't be involved, either, since he'd snow-shoed in, finding Eric en route. Then the two of them unwittingly had passed right by Aurora's body.

And, yes, I knew I hadn't put Eric on my list and I wasn't going to. So sue me.

But back to Naomi Verdeaux: she excused herself to go wash her hands, a little after

Aurora had gone out.

'I was in the bathroom.' Yeah, like we hadn't heard *that* excuse before.

Had she gone to Way's office looking for something? And then, as a result of what she'd found – or hadn't found – gone out looking for Aurora? Maybe she hadn't even intended to murder her.

Though that raised the question of murder weapon. Whoever had killed Aurora likely had gone outside with something deadly enough to cause the blow. Finding something outside, considering the two feet of snow on the ground, would be awfully tough.

Moving further down my array of cards, I saw that there were question marks next to Luc and Tien's names, too. I had no idea where they were when Way died. Tien, at least, had been in Goddard's the entire time Aurora was gone so she had an alibi for that murder. Luc, though, had returned to An's to get more fixings for the old-fashioneds. Or so he said.

Then there was Oliver.

I had to be honest. In addition to being a potential victim, he also had to be considered a suspect. With his parents dead, Oliver presumably would inherit the mall and everything else that Aurora and Way had.

I didn't know where Oliver was when his father was killed, but I needed to find out. As for Aurora's murder, Mrs G had said Oliver was making egg salad sandwiches and I had no reason to doubt her.

Except...

If Oliver and Mrs G were in it *together*, all bets were off. They could be lying for each other or, alternatively, one of them could have killed Way and the other Aurora.

Geez, I was suspecting kids and old ladies. What next?

Using the card display to pull myself up, I paused to wait for my right foot, gone to sleep from being tucked under me, to get feeling back. As I did, I scanned the area by the wood stove.

Eric was asleep – slumped forward, his head and arms draped over Frank, now sprawled across my son's lap. It looked awfully uncomfortable. I hobbled down the aisle toward them, wanting to rearrange the pair so Eric wouldn't get a crick in his neck. Like my nearly twenty-year-old was still a toddler, sleeping awkwardly in a car seat or a stroller.

However, knowing from past experience that both Eric and Frank would growl at me if I woke them up, I fought the impulse. Besides, other than the under-inflated beach balls, Frank was probably the best pillow in the place.

Mrs G and Sarah were still asleep in their lawn chairs, but when I turned to Oliver's, it contained Caron, face up and snoring. I hadn't seen Oliver leave or Caron arrive. Some sentry I was. I'd been so busy thinking about Oliver killing or *being* killed that I'd completely ignored him.

Even as I had the thought, though, I heard the hall door open. Oliver entered, carrying a book. As I watched, he slid it into the back of the book rack and picked up a magazine, flicking a cigarette lighter to try to read by its wavering light.

I went over and handed him my light-saber flashlight.

'Stir Wars?' he said, reading the side of it.

'It's a flashlight.'

He flicked the 'on' switch. 'It's a lighted swizzle stick.'

Oh.

'Well, it beats burning the place down with a cigarette lighter anyway,' I pointed out irritably. 'Use the swizzle stick.'

'You're not my mother,' Oliver protested, and then looked wounded.

'I'm sorry about your mom,' I said gently.

'Thanks.' He started to say something else but apparently thought better of it. He replaced the magazine on the rack, but backwards, with the rear cover facing out.

'Listen, Oliver. Since your mom and dad were...' I stopped, not knowing how much Oliver had been told by Sarah and the rest of the group while Luc, Rudy and I had been occupied moving the bodies.

'Murdered?' Oliver turned his attention back to me.

I cleared my throat. 'Yes. Since they were murdered, we all need to be careful. Not go off by ourselves.'

He turned red. 'I was just in the bathroom.'

Consistent with carrying the book as toilet reading. 'I know. Just be careful, OK? Someone here...'

I let it hang to see what his response would be. If Oliver inherited the strip mall, Mrs G could keep her business – *and* her home. And Oliver would keep the only place he'd called home as well.

'...is a killer,' Oliver finished, like he was accessing my thoughts. 'You think it was me?' He tossed down the Stir Wars light and pulled his lighter back out, along with a pack of cigarettes. Tapping one out, he lit it.

I pulled the cigarette out of his hands and stomped on it. 'No smoking.'

He went to take out another and I grabbed the pack and stomped on that, too. 'No smoking.'

He looked like I'd taken his ice cream cone away. 'Jesus, Maggy. My parents are dead, can't you cut me some slack?'

'You don't smoke, Oliver. You never smoked. And Mrs G would kill you if she saw you.'

'True.' He glanced uneasily toward the wood stove.

'So where were you when your father was looking for you to snow-blow?'

'Subtle.' He said it sarcastically, but answered anyway. 'I was here, helping Mrs G.'

Different time, but pretty much the same alibi. Sans sandwiches.

'I assume when your father couldn't find you, he started to clear the snow himself.'

'He must have.' Mrs G's voice came from behind me. Oliver surreptitiously flicked out his foot, sending the crushed pack of cigarettes skidding under the edge of the counter.

'I heard the snow-blower,' Mrs G continued. 'It started up just before I left for Uncommon Grounds. You were washing the

192

parsley, remember Oliver?'

Hmmm. The parsley defense. Not that it mattered. The important time was not when the John Deere was *started up*, but when it *stopped*.

'Were you still here when the snow-blower kicked out?'

Oliver glanced quickly over at Mrs G and then shrugged. 'I don't know exactly when that was, but I was here when Mrs G got back.'

Inconclusive, of course. Oliver could have killed Way and still been back in the pharmacy by the time Mrs G returned.

I left Oliver and Mrs G to a discussion of the eye strain that could arise from reading in dim light. Or maybe she was lecturing him on other ways to go blind.

While Naomi Verdeaux was still my preferred suspect, I wanted to interview her last, after I'd tied up the other loose ends.

One of those loose ends was Luc Romano. Where was he when the snow-blower coughed out?

I didn't see Luc anywhere, but I found Tien watching the storm through the 'GO' of 'Goddard Family Pharmacy' stenciled on the window. As I approached, the glass groaned under the force of the gale outside.

'That window is practically bowing, Tien. Should you be standing there?'

Honestly, who did I think I was? I'd gone from being just Eric's mom to overall mall-mother. Pretty soon I'd be cutting their meat into bite-sized pieces for them. If we had any meat.

But Tien turned, her face aglow. 'I know, but I just love storms. My father and I used to watch them together when I was little.'

'I did that with my mom, too,' I admitted. The two of us had stood in the open garage door, counting together. 'One one-thousand, two one-thousand...'

My mother – the squirrel, in this case, doesn't fall far from the tree – had taught me that each second that elapsed between our sighting the lightning flash and hearing the thunder meant the storm was another mile away.

It was only later that I tumbled to the fact that the speed of sound is only about a thousand feet per second, which means it takes about five seconds for the thunderclap to travel a mile. So, when Mom and I thought the lightning was still five miles from us, it was really only a mile away.

God knows how I survived my childhood. I'd gotten the math right with Eric, but he and I continued the tradition. Poking fun at each other when the thunder finally came and made us jump, Eric dashing out into the storm to play in the puddles, me laughing and telling him to be careful.

'The bigger the thunderstorm, the better,' I said, remembering.

Tien pointed out the window as the lightning strobed on the still falling snow. 'Is this one big enough for you?'

'And then some.' I sighed. 'I do prefer thunderstorms that you don't have to shovel.'

As I spoke thunder rumbled, following the lightning like ... well, thunder follows lightning. 'Is your dad sleeping?'

She shook her head, her dark hair swinging back and forth. 'I've never known my dad to sleep during a storm. I think he wants to keep watch. Make sure I'm safe.' She smiled, seeming a little embarrassed, but also proud that she had such a good protector.

'Take it from me. You never stop wanting to keep your kids safe.' I touched her shoulder. 'Whether they're two, or thirty-two.'

Her smile grew wider. 'I didn't get a chance to ask Eric. How does he like the U?'

Only students or locals called the University of Minnesota 'the U'. I cocked my head.

'Did you go to Minnesota? I don't know why, but I thought you went to UW in Madison.'

'I did,' Tien said, 'but I dated a guy who went to Minnesota. I put a lot of miles on my car driving up to The Cities to see him.'

The twin cities of Minneapolis and St Paul, Minnesota are about four hours from Madison, where the University of Wisconsin is, or five hours from Brookhills.

Take my word for it. I'd driven it behind the wheel of a rental truck for two autumns and one spring, taking Eric up and back.

'I bet you did,' I said. 'And Eric is doing great in Minneapolis.'

I was glad that I could say it honestly, given my fears about him earlier. 'He's a sophomore this year, so I don't hear from him as much as I used to.'

'That's a good sign. It means he's happy.' Tien nodded toward Oliver, who was sitting on the floor in front of the magazines, apparently willing to go blind. 'Life could be worse.'

'Like being brought up in a strip mall by uncaring parents who then go and get themselves killed?' I asked.

Tien, uncharacteristically, bristled at that. 'I don't think Way was uncaring. He was a very kind man.'

Aww, geez. Not another woman enthralled by Way Benson? I hoped Tien's name wasn't on the jerk's tattooed list of conquests.

I cleared my throat. 'So where did you say your dad was?'

Tien looked surprised at the turn of conversation. 'Talking to Rudy or more likely fighting with him. Over there.' She waved toward the 'Vitamin and Male Enhancement' aisle at the far end of the store.

'The two of them don't get along?' I asked. 'I can't say I ever noticed.'

Tien rolled her eyes. 'That's because sometimes they do and sometimes they don't. Honestly, think of five-year-old neighbor boys. You would think that being in the Army would give them something in common.'

'But no?' I could just catch sight of the two men's heads about five aisles down.

'Nope. In fact, it seems like a sore spot. It's too bad, really.' Her eyes grew sad. 'Dad could use a friend. It's not good for him to have just me to talk with, confide in – well, you know.'

Hmm. Might this be a veiled reference to the fact that Frank – admittedly a less than sterling conversationalist – was my closest companion?

Nah. But Tien's comment *was* a mirror image of what Luc had said to me, only about Tien.

I gave her a hug and went to see Luc and Rudy.

Interesting. Luc wanted Tien to branch out and she, him. I wondered if they'd ever talked to *each other* about it.

Then again, even if they had, it might be one of those impossible exchanges you run into between family members. Luc thinks Tien wants him to find friends beyond her, so *she* can be free. She assumes the same about him and suddenly we're in *Gift of the Magi* territory.

Happily, my family isn't that selfless. We're less 'I-cut-my-hair-to-sell-it-and-buy-you-something-you-no-longer-need' and more 'here's-your-gift-card'.

No confusion there. A gift certificate means never having to say you're sorry.

But as far as Tien and Luc's relationship, who knew? Maybe each *was* trying to do what he or she thought was best for the other. In the process, though, they'd please neither.

Honestly, I should have my own talk show. Solve the problems of the world. I could call myself Dr Maggy. Frank could be my sidekick, Ed McDogg. Tee-hee.

OK, OK, enough. God, I really could use some sleep. A dose of normality wouldn't hurt either.

As I approached Luc and Rudy, they turned to stare at me. Maybe it was because I was giggling maniacally, or maybe it was because they had something to hide.

The latter was borne out when, as I reached them, Rudy set the box he'd been holding on a shelf, and high-tailed it in the opposite direction.

NINETEEN

'I'm sorry,' I said, looking after Rudy. 'Did I upset him somehow?'

Luc shrugged. 'Nah, he probably doesn't want you to know he dyes his hair.'

I glanced at the shelf and saw 'Spruce-the-Goose Hair Dye For Men' misplaced on the shelf between herbal 'pick-me-ups' and condoms. 'Why don't they just package all three as "The Idiot's Guide to Getting Laid"?' I asked.

'Fischer's never needed any help in that department.' Luc said. It was a little bitter, but a little sad, too.

Tien was right. No fast friendship between these two.

Despite being stranded in the middle of a blizzard, with two bodies literally cooling their heels, I was curious. It wasn't like I had anything else to do, after all.

'Rudy's a ladies' man?'

Luc gave me a look like he was sorry he'd

said anything. His eyes also implied, though, that with some coaxing he might say even more. 'Maggy, you have no idea. And I'm not sure you want to.'

Oh, but I did. I really, really did. I'd rarely seen Rudy and Luc interact at all and now, it seemed, they had a history I didn't know about. That couldn't be tolerated.

'Please?' I pleaded.

'It was a long time ago.' Luc glanced toward the window where his daughter had been. 'I know that I should forget about it, but whenever I see him talking to Tien...'

I waited for Luc to go on, but he didn't. 'What was a long time ago?'

'Vietnam.' Luc turned to face me straight on.

'You and Rudy were stationed together?' Ignorance (or at least feigning it) sometimes *is* bliss.

Luc nodded. 'Rudy was already in-country when I got shipped over. And he had a real bad reputation.'

'For being a ladies' man?' I ventured.

Luc laughed, but with the bitterness really shining through now. 'That's a polite way to put it. I'd call him a pimp.'

Amazing what a can of worms a couple of murders and a brandy old-fashioned can open. 'Like the Mechanic in *Miss Saigon*?'

Luc showed a brief flash of anger. 'Without the singing and dancing.'

I waited.

Luc outwaited.

I finally gave in. 'You can't leave it hanging out there like this, you know. You've just told me Rudy Fischer, barber and less-than-esteemed former Brookhills town chairman, is a pimp.'

'*Was* a pimp.'

'Was a pimp,' I conceded. 'You can either tell me what you're talking about, or I can try to find out.'

Just the ghost of a smile from Luc. It made me wonder whether we were verging on information about a ghost of another kind.

An.

The fictional character of the Mechanic in *Miss Saigon* was a Vietnamese man who prostituted Vietnamese women. An was a Vietnamese woman.

'Are you saying that Rudy...' I hesitated. '...procured women for other soldiers?'

'Other officers,' Luc said. His face was stony, like he couldn't allow himself to react. 'They paid better.'

The unasked question – or two unasked questions – hung between us. 'Umm, did you...'

I let it hang, not knowing if I was asking if Luc, himself, had ... partaken, or if An had been involved with the 'business'.

Luc shook his head. 'No, I wasn't one of Rudy's GI johns.'

'But does he know you remember him?'

'Of course, though he denies all of it.'

'I don't think I've seen the two of you argue – or even speak much – before today.' Astonishing what could be lurking beneath the surface of a relationship that had seemed fairly placid. Heck, who was I kidding? I didn't even know there *was* a relationship between Luc and Rudy.

'I try to keep my distance,' Luc confirmed. 'But I don't like Rudy sniffing around Tien. He's always had a thing for petite women – Asian in particular – and I don't want him getting any ideas.'

'But he's so much older,' I protested. 'Tien couldn't possibly be interested in him.'

As I said it, I thought about her reaction to my comment on Way Benson. Given Tien's close ties to her father and the loss of her mother so early, maybe she *was* attracted to older men. Still, a father fixation was one thing, a grandfather fixation a whole 'nother animal.

'You're right. Tien is smarter than that. Still, I don't like Rudy or any of the other men around here setting their sights on her.'

Interesting. Despite what Luc had told me about Tien deserving a life of her own, he seemingly couldn't let her live it. I wondered if 'Dad' had seen the same thing in his daughter's eyes that I did when she talked about Way.

While the issue of An and Rudy's 'relationship', if any, hadn't been resolved, I couldn't see a subtle way to raise it again. So, instead I cleared my throat. 'I hate to put this to you, but I've been asking everyone. Where were you when Way died?'

'Me?' Luc looked surprised. 'I don't know. When did it happen?'

I wasn't sure that "when the snow-blower went off" was precise enough. 'About three this afternoon.'

'That's easy,' Luc said. 'Tien and I were in our store doing inventory all afternoon. We need to see what else could be sold off to cover this month's rent.'

The deli – first under its earlier incarnation as 'Romano's' and then as 'An's' – had been passed down from mother to son and, Luc might have hoped eventually, to daughter. Now they were reduced to liquidating stock in order to make their final lease payment.

'I'm sorry, Luc,' I said, laying my hand on his arm.

He patted it. 'I'm sorry, too, Maggy. Sorrier than you can imagine.' He turned to join Tien at the window, leaving me standing in the male-enhancement aisle.

Spent, I moved one aisle over seeking comic relief. And I found it. Bernie Egan was in the toy aisle playing paddle ball.

'Hey, Bernie,' I said, sidling up to him.

He stopped, the rubber ball missing the wooden paddle. Fortunately, it couldn't go far because of the elastic band stapled to both. 'Dang.'

'Sorry,' I said.

'Not to worry,' Bernie said. 'I was only up to a hundred seventy-three.'

Only. 'It was good of you to come out here in the storm to check on us.'

Bernie started again, bouncing the ball dead center on the red bullseye of the paddle. 'And find your body?'

'It's not *my* body,' I protested.

He slid a sideways look at me. 'Not yet, anyway.'

Bernie and I went a long time back, even beyond my marriage to Ted. In fact, Bernie had introduced me to my ex, which meant the pudgy lawyer and husband of my business partner had a lot to answer for, though I'd long ago forgiven him.

'Are you saying you want to kill me or that somebody else might?' I asked. The former was pretty much a given for most of my friends, most of the time.

Bernie bounced the ball once, twice, thrice, before stopping a second time. He was looking far more serious than usual. 'Honestly, Maggy?'

I nodded.

'You're becoming a magnet for trouble.'

'Me?' I said, surprised.

'You,' he said, starting up with the paddle ball again. 'I've been an attorney for twenty years and I haven't seen as many bodies as you have in the last two.'

'You're a copyright lawyer,' I pointed out. 'I'm not sure that's a fair comparison.'

'To a coffeehouse owner?' Bernie asked, one eye still on the ball.

He had a point. Coffee was not viewed as a commodity that inspires crime, at least not in Brookhills.

I decided to turn the spotlight on him. 'Why *did* you snow-shoe all the way here? Were you worried about what Caron might be doing?' I lifted my eyebrows.

He met my eyebrow-lifting and raised me an eye-roll. 'You're thinking I suspected Caron was somehow taking advantage of this paralyzing snowstorm to hook up with someone? Why would you even say that?'

Because I was a realist. An observer of life. A student of history. OK, a sicko. I shrugged. 'Dunno. Just asking.'

'If it's any of your business,' Bernie said, still not missing a beat with the paddle, 'I couldn't get hold of Caron by phone and wanted to let her know her doctor's office had called and cancelled her appointment for this afternoon.'

'They called her on her cellphone,' I told him. 'Besides, not only did you arrive hours after her appointment, but don't you think she would have figured out the appointment was off?' I pointed toward the ceiling, which was groaning from the wind and the snow.

'Probably, but ... I wanted to see her. Make sure she was OK.'

'Is she? I mean medically?' I asked, belatedly concerned. What a good friend I was.

'Oh, sure,' Bernie said. 'But I knew she'd be disappointed about missing the procedure.'

Procedure. Ahh. 'A plastic surgeon?'

'Breast Enhancement.' Bernie nodded and

set down the paddle to show how big.

'You're OK with this?' I asked. More than one aging Brookhills Barbie had let her Ken pay for a new set of bazzooms, only to divorce him for a younger man. Helllooooo Mrs Robinson.

Gave one hope for the future. Though it apparently was not the case with Caron and Bernie.

'You bet. And the blonde hair is great, don't you think?' Bernie enthused, setting his ball-and-paddle on the shelf.

'Like getting a new wife without the divorce,' I agreed, picking up the ball and squeezing it.

'Exactly right.' Bernie stroked the top of his head. 'I'm considering dying my hair – get rid of the gray. What do you think?'

What I thought was that if he didn't glue cotton balls to the top of his head there wasn't going to be much to dye.

'Rudy does his,' I evaded. 'Maybe you should ask him what he uses.'

'Great idea,' Bernie said, looking past me. 'I think that's him chatting up that Verdeaux woman. She's quite the hottie.'

'She is that,' I said, turning to glance their way. Rudy, indeed, was talking to Verdeaux, but both of them seemed angry. 'That looks more like bad blood than hot blood,' I said to Bernie.

'To some people, pleasure is business, instead of the other way around,' Bernie said, this time giving me back the arching eyebrows.

At five foot six, balding and perennially paunchy, Bernie wasn't exactly a sex symbol. I'd wondered over the years, though, if I'd have been better off with Bernie the Likeable Lawyer than with Ted the Duplicitous Dentist.

And, in the case of Naomi Verdeaux, Bernie might be right. According to Jacque, his ex-wife wasn't above bedding someone to get what she wanted.

Which reminded me. 'Do you know where Jacque is?' I asked.

Bernie shrugged. 'Got me. Here comes his former missus, though. I'm going to go ask Rudy about his hair while I have the chance.'

'You do that,' I said, wanting a chance to talk to Verdeaux myself.

'Got a second?' I said as she passed by me.

She laughed. 'Time is all I've got,' she said rubbing her bare arms. 'Damn Aurora for taking my coat.'

Not to mention getting killed in it. 'Maybe she thought it was tit for tat,' I said.

'Twit for what?' Naomi asked.

'No, no. *Tit* for tat. It means ... oh, never mind.' I figured 'tit' would be even tougher to explain than 'twit'. 'What I meant was maybe Aurora figured since you took her husband, she'd take your coat as revenge.'

'Believe me on this one,' Verdeaux said. 'The coat was worth more.'

I wasn't surprised to hear that from her, given Jacque's earlier evaluation. Of Verdeaux, not Way.

Still, I made my eyes widen in surprise. 'Really? Way was...' I hesitated. '...*legendary* around here.'

'Legendary pain in the butt, as far as I'm concerned,' Verdeaux said. 'We were all set with this deal and he starts listening to his ex-wife. Tell me something, who does that?'

'A man who still loves her?' I hazarded.

'Pfft,' she said, continuing down the aisle and around the corner to the stationery section.

I scurried after her. 'Pfft?'

Verdeaux had stopped at my digs and picked up my tablecloth. 'Pfft. As in, Way didn't love anyone. Except maybe that kid of his.'

'Oliver?' I was too surprised at what she'd said to stop her from wrapping herself up in

210

Sponge Bob. 'Way barely paid attention to him.'

'Pfft,' Verdeaux said again.

I wanted to smack her one. For both the 'pfft' and the tablecloth.

'That son of his? A crazy,' she continued, 'but Way still insisted he be allowed to work here at the plaza. Even after Gross National Produce and I took over the place.'

Interesting. Way apparently had cared about Oliver. Or at least he didn't want to risk having to support him.

Verdeaux pulled off the tablecloth and dumped it back on the floor. 'This is worthless,' she said. 'I want my coat.'

'Go and strip it off Aurora's body,' I said, deadpan. 'It's in Luc's freezer. Now, why do you say Oliver is "a crazy"?'

Verdeaux shivered. That would teach her to diss Sponge Bob. 'You're kidding, right? He's like that Ted Kaczynski, the Unabomber guy, except he lives in a shopping mall instead of a cabin. Keeps to himself. The only thing I've seen the kid wear is that camouflage sweatshirt. The one with the hood. He had it on today – or maybe yesterday, by now – when he was *snow-blowing*, for God's sake. You think that's not crazy?'

'I think it's being a teen...' I stopped. 'Wait

a second. Oliver was snow-blowing? Not Way?'

'Way? Snow-blow?' Verdeaux looked shocked. 'He couldn't even change a light bulb.'

It might be true, I guessed. I'd certainly never seen Way change a light bulb. 'You are absolutely sure it was Oliver snow-blowing? You saw him?'

'Of course I *saw* him. He was clearing the sidewalk just past your shop when I circled the lot the first time to see if Way was in his office.'

'And you say Oliver was wearing his hooded sweatshirt?' I couldn't even imagine it in the midst of the snowstorm. Then again, I had a teenaged son, too, and I knew what it took to get him to put on a jacket. Eighteen inches of snow would be just about right. 'Did Oliver have the hood up?'

'He did.' Verdeaux just looked at me.

'So how do you know it was him?' I asked triumphantly. It was an 'aha!' moment, and I don't have a lot of them.

Verdeaux shook her head and walked by me, treading on Sponge Bob as she did. 'Because the hood blew down as he turned the corner.'

So much for 'aha'. This felt more like 'uh-oh'.

'Wait,' I said. 'Which corner?'

'The one right by your store,' Verdeaux said impatiently.

'But that's not far from where Way's body was found.'

'With the snow-blower.' Verdeaux was speaking slowly and distinctly, like she was talking to a moron. Which, arguably, she was.

'You're suggesting that Oliver killed Way?' I asked. 'But why didn't you say something earlier?'

Verdeaux shrugged. 'Unlike you, I thought I'd let the police handle it. I *am* stuck here with him, you know.'

'But what about Aurora? Even if Oliver hated his father, I think he genuinely cared about his mother.'

'Oh, I do, too,' Verdeaux said, pausing at the corner. 'But maybe Oscar didn't intend to kill her.'

'Oliver,' I automatically corrected. 'And what do you mean that he didn't intend to kill his mother? You think he bashed her in the head by accident?'

'Of course not. The kid saw Aurora wearing my coat and thought it was me. Pfft.' A dismissive wave of her hand. 'After all, I *was* the one boffing his father.'

TWENTY

It was true, of course. Naomi Verdeaux was 'boffing', as she put it, Way Benson.

She wasn't the only one, though. Not now, nor over the last few years.

Yet Aurora had been wearing Verdeaux's coat. Who had known about that?

The answer was simple: anyone who had been in Goddard's when Aurora donned the coat and went outside.

But who was 'anyone'?

My name badge chart told me who had left Goddard's long enough to kill Aurora outside. What it didn't tell me was who was in Goddard's at the moment she'd stormed out.

I tried to think.

I'd been talking to Verdeaux, of course, after her argument with Aurora. Both of us had watched Way's widow leave. I also had a memory of Luc and Caron being around. I honestly wasn't sure who else, if anyone, was.

Because it made my head hurt, I set that question aside in favor of a more intriguing one.

Verdeaux said Oliver had on his camouflage sweatshirt. That, in itself, wasn't a surprise. He wore the shirt virtually everywhere. What *was* a surprise was that Oliver didn't have it on now. He'd been wearing a long-sleeved flannel shirt when he'd arrived at the scene of his father's murder. I remembered it clearly because his face seemed to match the green of his shirt when he'd looked down at Way's body. I thought he might be sick.

So where was the hooded sweatshirt now? Could it be hanging up somewhere, drying out from the snow? Or from his father's blood?

Intriguing question number two: If Oliver had been wearing the sweatshirt – which, like most of Eric's 'favorite' clothes, was nearly threadbare from washing – how had he managed to hide something as bulky as a cleaver or hatchet under it?

And, speaking of washing, the clattering sounds in the kitchen indicated that someone was doing their best to clean up the dishes from dinner even without running water. Since Oliver had abandoned the magazine rack and Mrs G was nowhere in sight, I assumed they were in the kitchen.

The perfect opportunity to talk in private.

As I stuck my head in, I saw Oliver waiting to scrape a pile of egg salad into the garbage. Mrs G was attempting to shove something already in the trash bin farther down in order to make room.

'Wait!' I cried, just as Oliver dumped the egg salad. I peered into the trash container. Ugh. Camouflage, a la egg salad.

As Oliver and Mrs G backed off, I grabbed a plastic glove from a box on the sink. Slipping it on, I gingerly reached in and pulled out the sweatshirt. In addition to the egg, mayo and a little chopped onion and pimento, the shirt was spattered with dark brown teardrops.

'Does one of you want to explain this?' I asked, dangling the shirt in front of them.

Oliver was looking down at the floor like Frank as a puppy after being caught in a puddle of his own piddle. 'I ... I...' He looked up hopefully. 'Cut myself?'

'C'mon,' I said, 'we all know that DNA testing will show this is blood all right, but not yours.'

'Don't be so sure,' Mrs G said. 'I think a

lab will find the alleles in common with Oliver here.'

Alleles? *Alleles?*

Apparently, Mrs G was a closet CSI fan.

Well, two could play that game. 'Certainly they will, because Oliver is Way's son and this –' I raised the sweatshirt dramatically and a glob of egg salad fell on to my shoe – 'is Way's blood.'

It looked like Mrs G was going to argue the point, but Oliver interrupted. 'I didn't kill him.' His eyes filled with tears. 'At least I don't think I did.'

'Of course you didn't kill him,' Mrs G said, coming up and putting her arm around him. 'He was already dead.'

I wasn't so sure, given all the blood sprayed around the John Deere at the scene, but I wanted them to keep talking. 'Your father was dead when you got there?'

Oliver nodded, relieved, I thought, to finally be able to tell his side of the story. 'After I cleaned off the sidewalk and the first row of parking on your side, I went around the corner, like toward the service entrance? I saw something sticking out of the snow and figured it was the handle of a shovel.'

'Something you'd no doubt be blamed for leaving out, knowing that father of yours,'

Mrs G added, shaking her head.

Objection. Leading the witness.

But Oliver just shrugged. 'Probably. So I snow-blowed over to pick it up, but before I got close enough to reach it...' He held up his hands in front of his face and closed his eyes, as though remembering the moment. Or, more likely, trying not to. Good luck with that.

I was buying Oliver's version, since I'd also thought the handle of the cleaver was a shovel nearly buried in the snow. The position of Way's body, head pointing toward the snow-blower, supported it, too.

'What did you do?' I asked.

'Do?' Oliver's eyes were wide now. 'I didn't know what I'd hit, but I figured it had to be something big. A fox, maybe, or even a coyote, on account of there being blood everywhere. So I put the John Deere in reverse and backed up. That's when I saw it was ... was...'

I knew that Pavlik, in my place, would keep quiet and let Oliver finish the sentence, hoping he would reveal more in his struggle to explain what he'd seen and how he'd felt about it.

However, I'm not Pavlik. 'So you realized it was your dad. What did you do then?'

Oliver looked at Mrs G. 'Freaked. And ran straight here to Goddard's.'

'That's true,' she confirmed. 'He was hiding right over there when I got back from your place.'

I followed her pointing finger to the corner beyond the trash barrel. Coming back to both of them, I said, 'Then why didn't you say anything? You had to know it would all play out eventually.'

Mrs G answered indignantly. 'Not if you kept your nose out of it. The boy *didn't do anything.*'

She punctuated the last three words using her pointing finger to poke my chest. The imposing old lady stood toe-to-toe and nearly nose-to-nose with me, her flowered dress billowing in contrast to my navy-blue tights, oversized T-shirt and fuzzy socks.

A catfight seemed less than prudent. And a lot ridiculous.

'So what did you do next?' I asked meekly.

Mrs G took a step back, but fixed me with an I'm-keeping-an-eye-on-you glare. 'I gave him one of Mr G's long-sleeved flannels from the Goodwill box and took the sweatshirt from him. Before I could get rid of it, Jacque came looking for flashlights and something to eat.'

'Wait a second, wait a second,' I said, holding up my hands.

Mrs G started to wag her pointing finger at me, but I was having none of it.

'You have a Goodwill box with flannel shirts in it and you gave me just this thin T-shirt –' I did a pirouette – 'to wear?'

'They're Hank's clothes,' she said tightly.

'Wearing a man's clothes still would have been a whole lot warmer.'

'Nobody wears Hank's clothes.' She poked me in the chest again. '*No*body.'

Except, apparently, Oliver Benson, her surrogate grandson. Mrs G's unblinking stare and obstinate stance was starting to give me the heebie-jeebies. I hoped we wouldn't find Hank in a rocking chair somewhere, hunting rifle clutched in his skeletal hands.

I backed down again. 'OK, OK. I get that. No one wore Ted's clothes, either.'

'You divorced your husband,' she said, eyes narrowing.

'Damn right, and the minute he was out of sight, I burned anything he'd left behind that would catch fire.' So, come to think about it, not even *Ted* got to wear Ted's clothes.

Mrs G seemed all right with that. 'I was going to burn Oliver's sweatshirt, too,' she admitted. 'That's why I started the fire in the woodstove. But, like I said, when Jacque came in, I had to throw the thing into the trash and leave it here.'

As with Oliver's version, Mrs G's made sense to me.

Then she shrugged. 'I figured we'd dump egg salad on top of the sweatshirt and pitch the bag so no one would be the wiser.'

'Except you, now,' Oliver said to me.

I gauged him carefully to see if the words had been a threat, but he just looked glum.

'The snow-blower wasn't running when I found your father's body,' I said to him. 'Did you turn it off?'

Oliver shook his head. 'No. When I hit ... umm...'

'Your father's body,' Mrs G prompted.

'Yeah.' Oliver looked grateful he didn't have to say the words himself. 'Anyway, the auger jammed, so the engine cut out.'

I'd heard the John Deere's engine die when I was in Uncommon Grounds. Rudy had come in looking for gas for the generator and I remembered thinking that the snow-blower must have run out of gas, too.

I'd assumed, as everyone else had, that it was Oliver clearing the snow. It was only after I'd found Way dead next to the machine that I had jumped to the conclusion he'd been the one operating it.

Which meant I'd been right in the first place, and just didn't know it.

Cold comfort.

I shivered and rubbed my arms. 'Did you see your dad this morning?'

'No. Well, at least not until...' Oliver hesitated. '...the accident. I'd gotten a text message from Mom saying he was ticked because he couldn't find me. That he wanted to keep the parking lot cleared as the snow fell so cars could get in and out.'

You could say lots of things about Way, most of them unflattering, but he did do what he could to keep us in business and paying rent. Until he kicked us out.

It occurred to me, suddenly, that I didn't know which of Oliver's parents he lived with. I asked him.

'Both,' he said. 'Like some nights I stay with my dad, other nights with my mom.'

Aurora had said Way called her looking for Oliver. 'So you weren't at your father's place last night?'

'No, it was my mom's turn.'

'But you weren't there, either,' I said with all the 'mom-ness' a mother could muster.

It worked. He turned red. 'I ... umm, I stayed with friends.'

That felt right, too. The next question I'd ask Eric was which friends.

But I wasn't Oliver's parent. In fact, nobody was anymore.

'And when you got here?' I asked, my voice softening. 'You didn't see your father when you took out the snow-blower?'

The machine and other maintenance items were stored in the dumpster corral about thirty yards from the rear service door.

'Uh-uh.' Oliver shook his head. 'I was trying to avoid him because I knew he'd give me shit – sorry, grief – for not answering his calls. I just went straight to the corral and wheeled the thing out.'

'Then, could your father have been lying near the service door already?'

Oliver seemed to think about it. 'Maybe, Mrs Thorsen. You see, I went straight from the corral to the parking lot and did the front row of that and your sidewalk. Then I went back around the building toward the service door.'

I said, 'Did you hear anything?'

A glimmer of a smile. 'Not over the four-cycle engine of the John Deere I was pushing.'

Maggy, you're an idiot. 'OK, did you *see* anything?'

223

'Just the ... the...'

'Shovel handle,' Mrs G said, giving his shoulder a squeeze. 'And that's enough for now.' A fierce – fiercely protecting, like unto murderous – stare at me.

It *was* enough, not just because I believed Oliver and felt sorry for what he'd been through. I also needed time to mull over this new information, especially on the sequencing of events. Not to mention that Mrs G was continuing to give me the creeps.

I nodded stiffly and left the kitchen, stopping by the wood stove's guttering fire to warm myself.

Once I had assumed – wrongly – that Way was the one snow-blowing and the John Deere's engine had stopped when it chopped up his head. I'd been right about the last, at least.

Thing is, though, by the time Oliver stumbled on Way, he already was on the ground with a hatchet in his back. And, enough new snow had fallen to hide the body, if not the 'shovel handle'.

But which had actually killed Way? The meat cleaver? Or the snow-blower? The medical examiner would have the answer. But only eventually.

Either way, though, the collision with Way's

head must have been an accident. For Oliver's sake, I hoped his dad was dead when the boy hit him. If Way hadn't been, though, I imagined he was bleeding out and well on his way to freezing to death already.

But enough cheery thoughts. Back to what I once heard our Sheriff Pavlik call the 'objectivity of chronology'.

The new information meant my timeline was wrong. I needed to figure out *not* who was unaccounted for at the exact moment the snow-blower had cut out. No, I had to find out who didn't have an alibi for the period of time between Way starting the generator and when Oliver had found his body.

Time to reshuffle my name badges.

TWENTY-ONE

As I stepped into my dead-end aisle, I saw Frank at the far end.

His head popped up and he looked overjoyed to see me.

This posed a problem, since my aisle-wide suspect chart was between us.

How Frank had gotten to the opposite end of the aisle, I didn't know. Levitating – along with sit, stay, down and fetch – was not in his doggy bag of tricks.

However he did it, though, I wouldn't bet on his duplicating the feat with his big furry feet.

'Stay,' I tried, knowing it was useless. Worse than useless. His tail-stump was wagging furiously and he was jumping forward and back, pawing at the ground like he was about to charge.

I held up both hands and stepped carefully over the badges, managing to displace one Aurora and a pair of Jacques. As I approach-

226

ed Frank his excitement grew.

'Good dog. What a good, *good* doggie you are,' I said. I didn't want to ask a leading question like: 'Do you have to go out?' since that would send him into a frenzied stampede toward the closest door.

'Gotta go out, Frank?'

Eric's voice came from the front of Goddard's.

'Shhh,' I tried, but it was too late.

Frank put down his head and charged, fur flopping, legs churning. I could only flatten myself against the cabinet and watch helplessly as he skidded toward my chart.

I blinked.

Frank was gone. I could hear Eric talking to him at the door. And my chart was still intact.

Now how had he done that? Just the breeze off his flopping ears alone should have sent everything flying.

Not one to look a gift-dog in the mouth, I settled down on the floor. Happily, the 'Aurora's Death' portion of my chart could remain as it was. Just Way's section would be affected by the new fact he had died earlier than I had guessed.

The only person whose whereabouts I could be absolutely certain of, besides myself and Eric, was Caron. My partner had been in the store with me and, though I didn't give much credence to 'crisscross' alibis that two other suspects – like Oliver and Mrs G – provided each other, I had plenty of respect for my own.

As for Sarah ... I looked at my chart. Now where did I put our real-estate broker's badge?

Nowhere. Great. I couldn't even remember all the suspects. Not that I really considered Sarah a suspect. Still, she'd been there and fair was fair.

I pulled out my last two badges and settled once more on to the floor. On one, I wrote Sarah's name. Then I leaned back on the card cabinet as I thought about her alibi for Way's murder.

She'd initially been with Caron and me in Uncommon Grounds, but left to walk to her office just before I went home for Frank. I was certain, though, that Sarah had returned before Way started the generator and remained there until Oliver had found his father's body.

As for the time frame of Aurora's death, I'd seen Sarah in Goddard's and couldn't remember her leaving the pharmacy. Since I hadn't noticed Oliver's exit either, though, I couldn't be sure.

I put Sarah's whereabouts for both Way's and Aurora's deaths on my last badge. No need to break the bank by buying another eight-pack.

Then I started at the top of the list and edited the badges below as needed. Naomi Verdeaux had arrived at UG just after the snow-blower stopped. That meant she had no alibi for the period before that. I inked in 'NO ALIBI'.

On the other hand, the change in the timeline helped exonerate Jacque, who'd left the coffee shop just before Oliver found the body, but otherwise was with us there the rest of the morning, except when he was running his car into the ditch that first time or mowing Frank and me down, the second.

Rudy's badge was pretty much the same. He'd arrived at UG looking for more gasoline for the generator just after Way started it and Rudy stayed throughout.

I stood up and held my paper lantern at arm's length so I could see the whole chart.

Hi! My Name is Suspects	Hi! My Name is Way's Death	Hi! My Name is Aurora's Death
Caron Egan	With Maggy in UG	With Maggy in Goddard's
Aurora Benson	Had just left UG in search of Way	Dead
Naomi Verdeaux	Arrived at UG just after snow-blower goes silent NO ALIBI	In Way's restroom, supposedly, then at Goddard's
Jacque Oui	~~Goddard's? Had just left UG~~ IN UG FROM TIME WAY STARTED GENERATOR TO JUST BEFORE BODY FOUND	In Goddard's
Oliver Benson	? GODDARD' THEN SNOW-BLOWING	Making egg salad with Mrs G
Mrs G	~~In UG~~ GODDARD'S THEN UG	Making egg salad with Oliver
Rudy Fischer	~~In UG when snow-blower stops~~ AT UG FROM JUST AFTER WAY STARTED GENERATOR, UNTIL AFTER SB STOPPED	Getting brandy old-fashioned mixings
Luc Romano	? AN'S	Gone to get more drink mixers

230

Tien Romano	~~?~~ AN'S	In Goddard's
Bernie Egan	Home	On his way to Goddard's – found Eric, saw body
Sarah Kingston	UG	Goddard's?

A drop of dirty slush fell on Oliver's name.

I looked up, trying to see where the water had come from, and got hit in the face with another plop. Wiping it off, I peered up, but the dangling paper lantern in my hand wasn't providing any upward illumination.

'Does anybody have a flashlight?' I called. 'I'm afraid we might have a problem with the roof.'

'A what?' Mrs G was awake, out of her chair and wringing her hands before anyone else could reply. 'But the roof has been fine. Always.'

Because Benson Plaza had a flat roof, snow couldn't easily slide off as it does from a pitched roof. Over the length of a winter, Way might send a crew up to the roof once or twice to shovel it off. I'd never, though, seen this much snow – and heavy, heavy snow – fall so quickly. To add to the problem, the first snow that fell was insulated by the subsequent snow on top, as well as the warm roof below. This meant that bottom snow melts, meaning...

'A leak?' Mrs G sounded like she wanted to command it away. 'My ceiling doesn't leak.'

It does now.

Luc and Rudy started to approach the mouth of my aisle from opposite ends with their flashlights. Seeing each other, both stopped. Jacque, followed by Sarah, pressed by Luc and directed his flashlight beam up.

'Uh-oh,' said Sarah.

Uh-oh was a reasonable, though not very specific, assessment. Even I could see that the ceiling tiles were sagging.

Luc came up behind Sarah. 'This isn't good.'

'Will these buckets help?' Mrs G asked. She had two sand pails from aisle three. They had pink shovels attached, and looked appropriately pint-sized. Oliver and Eric were standing behind her. Each had an inflatable kid's swimming pool, still in its box.

Luc shook his head. 'They'll catch some dripping, but the water itself isn't the problem.' He surveyed the place in a hurry. 'This part of the 'L' is the original mall. The other side was added later. If the tiles we can see are sagging, the old roof above them is already going.'

'Going where?' Mrs G asked.

'Down,' Rudy said, having joined the party. 'Luc is right. We should get out of here.'

'It doesn't look a whole lot safer out there,' Sarah said, pointing out the window. As if she had summoned the gods a rumble of thunder sounded.

'Pfft.' Naomi Verdeaux had arrived. 'Some of us don't even have coats.'

'I didn't mean leave the mall,' Rudy said. 'We just need to get to the newer part of the building.'

Luc nodded. 'Your barbershop would be best,' he said to Rudy, feud apparently forgotten during an emergency.

'You're right,' Rudy said. 'The corner should have the most support.'

I didn't get where all this sweetness and light between the two of them was coming from, but if warring factions could agree, I stood ready to get in line behind them.

'But we just can't leave my shop like this,' Mrs G said, carefully setting one of the pails under one of the drips. 'I'll have a flood.'

'We can blow these up,' Oliver said, stepping forward. He'd removed one of the pools from its box and was shaking it out, looking for the inflation valve. 'Then...'

The ceiling panel behind him caught my attention. I grabbed his arm and pulled him toward me, sweeping Mrs G along with him.

'Hey,' he protested. 'What—'

He was interrupted by the giant ceiling tile, which I'd seen bowing badly, crashing to the floor, followed by a gush of water and slush. The tiles around it were leaning, too, as if being sucked in.

Eric and I looked at each other across the breach.

'We have to get out of here now,' Rudy commanded. Whatever his past might have been, he knew how to take charge. And, right then, I was grateful for that quality in him.

Everyone obeyed. Those of us who were under the falling sections quicker than those who weren't. Eric reached out and took my hand, steadying me as I crossed the debris in the aisle. Oliver and Mrs G followed.

Verdeaux, Jacque and Sarah made a beeline for the door with Rudy leading the way. Luc awakened Tien, who was at the far end of the store and followed. Mrs G was going in the other direction, Oliver trying to chase her down.

'There's a fire in the wood stove,' she said. 'We can't leave it unattended.'

Though I had no intention of staying to

watch a fire that soon would be engulfed in snow, I understood the desire to protect what you have left.

'I'll knock down the fire,' I told Oliver and Eric. 'You get Frank and take him and Mrs G to Rudy's.'

I was appealing to the two's protective instincts. A boy and his dog, and a boy and his surrogate grandmother.

Oliver nodded and turned away, his arm trying to guide Mrs G. She deflected him long enough to grab her handbag and check the cash register. 'All right, now I'll go.'

As they left, Oliver turned back to me. 'Thank you,' he said. He was looking worn, but not quite defeated. Yet. The events of the last few hours would take their toll later, I knew from personal experience. I selfishly was glad the reaction was delayed, since it kept Oliver a functioning human being. We needed all of those we could get.

My ploy wasn't quite as successful with Eric.

'I'm not going anywhere without you,' he said. Frank sat firm behind him.

It's nice to be loved. Most of the time.

The stove was throwing out minimal heat as we got there. The newspapers Eric and I brought over had long ago been reduced to ash and all that remained of a nest of wooden school rulers was a teepee of the thin metal strips that had edged them.

Eric opened the fire screen and used the poker to separate the elements of the fire even farther. A whimper sounded behind me.

I turned, expecting to see Frank impatient to be out of there.

Instead, there were Caron and Bernie crammed on to one of the chaise lounges sound asleep. As I looked, Caron moaned in her sleep and ran her hand up and down Bernie's back. Bernie roused and pulled her closer.

'Oh for God's sake,' I muttered to Eric. 'We're in the midst of a blizzard with the roof caving in and these two are making nanookie of the north?'

Eric laughed and Frank, ever happy to lend a paw, began to bark.

Bernie rolled off the side of the lounge, landing hard on the linoleum floor.

'Whaa?' he said.

'The sky is falling, Chicken Little.' I put my hand down to help him up. 'Roust your honey and get yourselves down to Rudy's.'

To his credit, Bernie quickly realized what was happening and began shaking Caron's shoulder.

I told Eric to lead everybody out and this time he obeyed. Frank padded after them, and I promised to be on their heels, after I checked the aisles.

All clear of people, at least. I stopped in the card aisle, ruefully surveying my forlorn alibi chart half-covered by the fallen ceiling. My Sponge Bob tablecloth was on the floor in 'Toys'.

I hesitated, thinking that Rudy's shop wouldn't be any warmer. Decision made, I leaned down to snatch the tablecloth. As I did, there was a loud groan. I looked heavenward and managed to jump back just before the ceiling crashed down, raining wood, acoustic tiles and shingles.

Poor Sponge Bob, I hardly knew ye.

Turning, I ran for the exit, the pharmacy's roof – and Gloria Goddard's dream – collapsing behind me.

TWENTY-TWO

Even the emergency lights were out when I entered the service hallway. Luckily someone, maybe Eric, had the forethought to leave a paper lantern to light my way. Either that, or someone had dropped it in his or her haste.

The long part of the 'L' of Benson Plaza was, as Luc said, the original building. The side Uncommon Grounds was on – the bottom of the 'L' – had been added about twenty years later.

Accordingly, Rudy's Barbershop was a little of each. As the section that connected the two wings of the mall, the corner juncture was doubly reinforced. Like a broken bone, once mended, is supposed to be stronger than that part of your skeleton before the trauma.

I'd never quite understood the broken bone thing, but I was willing to take a chance on the barbershop. Especially since the rest of the mall was falling down around us. I grabbed the lantern to light my progress and dashed down the hall. I could still hear a muffled crashing behind me in Goddard's, no doubt the heavy blanket of snow acting as both demolition charge and silencer.

Passing An's, I saw that the door was ajar. God, I hoped Tien or Luc hadn't taken shelter there, since I figured it was next to go. As I went to pull the door open to check, it swung wide in front of me.

'Luc,' I said, 'we have to get out of here.'

He was grasping an album. 'Photographs,' he said. 'They're all I have left of An.'

A crash behind him sheared off anything further by way of words. The images in the album might be the only tangible reminders Luc had left of his wife, but I feared that, in seconds, they'd also be all he had left of the store named after her.

Even worse, if we didn't evacuate immediately, pictures and memories might be all Tien had of Luc.

And Eric, of me.

Luc grabbed my hand and we bolted down the hall. Arriving gasping at Rudy's service door, I pulled down on the handle.

Locked.

I tried again. Ka-chink, ka-chink, but no

239

pay-off.

'Open up!' I pounded my fist on the metal above the lock.

Since the only light in the hallway was the one we carried with us, I couldn't see what was happening back down the hallway behind us. But I sure could hear it. Rolling thunder of the crumbling construction variety and it was marching closer.

I felt like I was a kid again and the bogey man was bearing down on me. 'Unlock the door, damn it!'

Luc reached past me, pushed down harder on the handle and yanked on the door, which now finally opened.

'Ladies, first,' he said as he ushered me in and closed the door behind us.

I could almost hear Ted, my ex, saying, 'Maggy, sometimes it just takes a man's touch.' This time he might be right, but so what? As that Austrian novelist Marie von Ebner-Eschenbach said way back when: even a stopped clock is right twice a day.

'Is everyone here?' I called. My hand was on the bolt of the door.

The moment everyone answered with their names, I locked us in. I wasn't sure why. Neither bogey men nor collapsing roofs likely would respect a deadbolt.

'Over here, Mom,' Eric called, 'by the sinks.'

I followed Eric's voice to the far wall, which the barbershop shared with The Bible Store. Until a few months ago, the store's space had been a dental office, the two hair-washing sinks in Rudy's paralleling the two spit-sinks on the other side.

The original tenant, Dr Anthony Bruno, had become my dentist after my dentist husband had run off with Little Miss Root Canal (his root, her canal). Then Tony retired and abandoned me, too.

'Can you stand back a little from that window?' I asked Eric. Even as I said it, I joined him and glanced out.

I don't know what I expected to see besides more snow, which we'd endured for what seemed like weeks instead of hours. I had to admit I was more than a little un-nerved by the cave-in develop—

BOOM!

'Geez.' I grabbed my son's arm. 'That sounded like a lightning strike nearby.'

Eric gave me a bemused look. 'I thought you liked thundersnow. Remember my report in the fifth grade?'

'Your "report" didn't forecast a ninety percent chance of falling ceilings and rising body counts.'

Eric just laughed, but now Sarah was peering out the window, too. 'It sounded like it hit down the road. Sure hope it was Schultz's instead of my place.'

Jacque, owner of Schultz's, shouldered her out of the way. 'What is it that you see?'

Naomi Verdeaux, who was sitting dejectedly in the chair in front of one of the sinks, clenched her teeth. 'I'm sure your precious store is fine. And if not –' she sat upright in the chair, as if a sudden thought had struck – 'you'll have the insurance money to replace it.'

'That is true,' from her ex-husband.

'Or maybe...' Verdeaux unfolded herself from the chair to sashay – and I don't use that term lightly – over to Jacque. '...build something ... bigger.'

She patted his shoulder.

Jacque turned his attention away from the window and regarded her hand suspiciously. 'You are suggesting perhaps a Gross National Produce?'

The patting had turned into kneading. 'You. Me. In business again, Jacque. Just like the old days. It would be great fun, no?'

The conniving woman had shed her Midwest accent and slipped into Jacque's way of speaking like a hermit crab worms its way into a new shell.

Rudy groaned. Had Way been alive, he'd probably have done likewise. There was a whole lot of groaning going on in Brookhills these days.

For his part, Jacque looked momentarily skyward and then shifted his eyes toward the display of antique straight razors on the back wall of the shop. Walking toward the carefully crafted artifacts, he said, 'Perhaps it is best that you slit my throat now.'

Jacque looked around for help. 'Would someone be so kind as to volunteer?'

Rudy shook his head. 'Not with my razors, Oui. My insurance premiums are too high already. You'll have to put yourself out of her misery.'

I started to giggle and then slapped my hand over my mouth. This was the time to listen, not make light of more violent deaths after the two murders our own little band had experienced.

It sure was fascinating, though. Jacque had been dead-on about Naomi Verdeaux. She used her body as a weapon. Or maybe 'currency' would have been more accurate.

Not being stupid *or* hard of hearing, Verdeaux gave up and stalked away in a definitely sashay-less manner.

Rudy and Jacque lowered their voices, so I sidled closer to hear, signaling Eric to stay put.

Rudy was shrugging. 'I really thought she was the one, old fool that I am.'

Truth be told, I doubted that Rudy considered himself either old or a fool, though the last several months probably had been tough on his usually well-inflated ego.

Just last year he'd battled my former business partner, Patricia, over the job of Brookhills town chairman. When Patricia died, Rudy, as the incumbent, had kept the job until a special election could be held. When Way beat him in the subsequent special election, it must have been a real blow to Rudy's self-image.

God knows I understood that. Ted left me the day after we took Eric up to the Twin Cities for college. With both of them gone, I decided, idiot that I was, to compound matters by quitting my long-time public relations job at First National Bank.

Take it from me, middle-age is not the best stage of life to figure out who you want to be when you grow up. That process is one best done, aided by wine, marijuana and peanut butter and onion sandwiches, twenty or thirty years earlier.

'It is not you my ex-wife desired,' Jacque was saying to Rudy, 'it is your lease. Naomi Verdeaux could not take over the entire building without your consent.'

Interesting, and not because Jacque spoke of her as 'Naomi Verdeaux'. For all I knew, that could be just a French thing.

It was interesting because while I knew that Rudy had been the 'make-or-break' tenant when the mall opened and therefore had gotten a sweeter deal than we latecomers, I didn't realize his original bargain gave him veto power of some kind.

Rudy was shrugging. 'I was planning on hanging up the clippers anyway, now that I'm free to travel. Leaving the position of town chairman was the best thing I could have done.'

He continued. 'I simply thought investing in Gross would be a good investment. A hobby of sorts.'

A hobby? More likely he'd hoped Naomi Verdeaux, the little whore, was going to be his 'hobby' for the next few years.

Hobby Whores – Brookhills' answer to the Chicken Ranch, the real-life brothel that *The Best Little Whorehouse in Texas* was based on. Maybe we could get our own movie, too.

Now *there* was a hobby for Rudy.

I snickered. Rudy and Jacque turned in my direction, so I ducked farther behind the coat rack at the door. Given there were no coats on it, though, it didn't provide much cover.

When they continued to stare at me, I cleared my throat. 'Just trying to keep warm.'

'Then you should move away from the door,' Rudy said. 'I've been after Way for years to put weather-stripping around it to get rid of the draft.'

Whine, whine, whine.

Half the mall had collapsed and we were trapped for the night with two bodies in a freezer that could be buried by morning under a couple of tons of ceiling panels, wooden joints and sodden shingles.

Oh, and our landlord, who'd been so unresponsive, was dead. Forgive and forget, eh?

As I saw it, we should be grateful the remainder of our group was safe, warm or not.

'Hey!' Sarah was digging in a basket. 'These look cozy.' She shook a blue smock out and hair went flying.

Served her right. I'd never heard Sarah use the word 'cozy'. Pretty soon she'd be 'quainting' and 'charming' us.

Then again, she *was* a real-estate agent.

'Hey, those are dirty,' Rudy said sourly, flicking a lock of hair off his nose. 'They're full of hair cuttings.'

Sarah looked at the oversized bib. 'Might make 'em warmer,' she said.

'Like a hair shirt instead of a fur coat,' Caron contributed from the couch in the waiting area.

She'd been paging through a copy of *Deer Hunting Today*, though she probably couldn't see a thing in the dim light. All the best, given that Caron had cried through *Bambi*. Four times. And *Lion King*, too, though the latter proved less of a problem, living in Wisconsin. One doesn't stumble across the King of Beasts very often.

'God, my head hurts,' she said now, putting the magazine down. 'Maybe a ceiling tile hit me as we ran.'

Or a maraschino cherry. I was about to point out that the brandy old-fashioneds were the more likely culprit, when a muffled sob drew my attention back to the sinks. Mrs G was in the second of the two chairs, sobbing softly. Oliver was on the floor next to her, talking earnestly to Eric.

As Eric shook his head, apparently in irritation at something Oliver had said,

Naomi Verdeaux stamped past them and right up to me.

'Did your partner say something about a fur coat? It's mine, you know, and I expect it back. She'd better not be getting any ideas about keeping it.'

Self-involved, thy name is Naomi Verdeaux. She made *me* look like Mother Teresa. But alive.

'First of all,' I said, 'if you want to know what Caron said, why don't you ask her?'

'I would, if she'd come up for air.' She pointed.

Caron had been joined on the couch by Bernie.

'Honestly,' Verdeaux said. 'What is with that woman? She's a worse slut than I am.'

'True,' I said, watching the canoodling. 'But only with her husband.' I didn't add: '*This* year.'

'As for the coat,' I said, turning back to Verdeaux. 'She wasn't talking about yours.'

'That's right,' Luc said, joining us. He had a paper cone cup from the water cooler in his hand. 'Your coat is still blood- and snow-molded around poor Aurora's body back in my freezer.'

Then, as Luc sipped from the cup, his eyes brightened. 'Hey, I have an idea.' He gestured toward the back hallway. 'Maybe you should go retrieve it. And take Rudy with you. He's good at stripping bodies.'

Apparently détente was over.

'Daddy, don't be rude,' scolded Tien from the windows where she'd resumed watching the storm.

Luc squeezed Verdeaux's shoulder and crossed to Tien. The rumbling of the storm had seemed to die out, or maybe it had been drowned out by the competing sound of the roof falling in. Now, though, it had resumed in earnest.

Luc stared out. Lightning flashed, and a boom followed immediately, meaning the storm was basically right overhead. 'Ahh,' he said, seeming transfixed, 'reminds me of the war.' He took another sip of water.

Tien regarded him suspiciously and then stuck her nose in the paper cup. 'Is that brandy? You don't drink.'

Luc, indeed, hadn't downed his old-fashioned at Goddard's. Caron had. Along with her own and everyone else's left unattended for more than ten seconds.

Caron, who'd been in a lip-lock with Bernie, dropped him cold. 'Brandy? Is there more? Maybe it would get rid of this headache.'

Right. 'Hair of the dog,' I muttered.

Frank, who was padding by, gave me a suspicious look.

'Not *your* hair,' I assured him and, seeming satisfied, he moved along.

Yet another reason why Frank was superior company to most humans I knew. He seldom required complex explanations. And he'd never sat down next to me with a 'Can we talk?'

Rudy picked up the bottle of brandy that was on the floor next to the water cooler. 'Found the open Korbel I was looking for, huh?'

He took a paper cone from the dispenser and poured some for himself, wisely ignoring Caron's pleas from the couch. 'You still think about Vietnam, Luc? The training? The wading through flooded rice paddies?'

'I do.' Luc took another slug. 'Though I can understand why *you* would want to put it out of your mind. And it has nothing to do with rice paddies.'

Rudy surveyed Luc sadly. 'A lot of us have memories we want to erase. Sometimes we try to do it with too much of that.' He nodded at the cup in Luc's hand.

Luc reddened in the glow of the nearby lime-green lantern. He crushed his half-full cone in his hand, sending brandy spritzing.

Naomi Verdeaux was in the line of fire. 'Jesus, can't you macho assholes act your age? Not only is my coat stolen from me, but now this silk blouse is ruined.' She wiped at same, furiously.

Rudy went to help her, but she swatted away his hand. 'Nice try,' she snarled. 'I'm cold and I'm wet, but you are the *last* person I want to warm me up. And though none of you apparently think it appropriate, even the person making the suggestion, I'm going to get my coat.'

She strode to the door, yanked on the handle and pushed hard twice before noticing the engaged deadbolt. Impatiently ramming it aside, she swept out into the back hallway, slamming the door behind her.

'Gee,' I said, injecting sisterly concern into my voice, 'I hope she didn't break a nail.'

After the laughter, weary as it was, subsided, Rudy shook his head. 'Don't underestimate that woman. I'm starting to think she's capable of anything.'

Including stripping her coat off a dead woman as the mall falls down around her?

'You're a fine one to talk,' Luc was saying. He was slurring his words a bit. 'You know what I've been thinking?' He moved unsteadily toward Rudy. 'I've been thinking that soldiers are really good at sneaking up on someone and sticking a knife in their backs.'

Rudy laughed. 'First you ruined my reputation by claiming I was a pimp way back when. Now you're suggesting that because I was in Vietnam, I'm the best candidate for killing Benson? What about you? You're a vet, too. And that thing sticking out of Way's body looks a whole lot more like a meat cleaver than –' he pointed at his wall display – 'a straight razor.'

The way things were going, it might be a good idea to gather up every sharp implement in the place and throw them into a snowdrift so no one could hurt anyone.

But then there were always bare hands.

Luc leapt at Rudy, moving far more steadily now than I would have expected, given the alcohol. Rudy stumbled back, nearly knocking the five-gallon water jug off the cooler.

I looked around for help in the form of a male, but Jacque seemed content to sit back and enjoy the show, while Bernie was ... otherwise occupied.

'You fucking pimp,' Luc said, advancing. 'You're accusing me of murder?'

Rudy put out both arms to fend him off. 'Every swinging dick in Saigon was having sex with the local girls. You did, too. The only difference was that I made sure the guys paid them something to live on.'

'Noble of you,' Luc sneered or at least tried to. He had one eye closed, looking like a drunken Popeye.

'More noble than you were,' Rudy replied. 'Do you think you did An a favor by taking her away from her family and then leaving her alone while you went to the bars? You didn't drink *yourself* to death. You drank *her* to death.'

Luc launched himself at Rudy again, this time taking down both him and the water cooler. The two of them wrestled on the floor, the five-gallon bottle lolling next to them, its water glug-glug-glugging all over the floor.

I grabbed Luc's shirt, trying to pull him off Rudy. They rolled and nearly took me down with them. Two other pairs of hands reached in and pulled the men apart.

I turned, expecting Jacque and Bernie. Instead, I saw Sarah and Tien. Tien had tears running down her face. Sarah looked like she just wanted to haul off and hit someone herself.

'You numbskulls,' she yelled. 'We're stuck in a blizzard with no way of communicating with the outside world. We have not one, but two, dead bodies stored in a meat freezer. And now the roof is falling in. Do you think you could possibly save this for another time?'

Tien was helping her father up. 'Are you OK, Daddy?'

Luc looked stricken. 'You know that I loved your mother, don't you?'

'Of course I do,' Tien assured him. 'We can talk about this later, OK?' She swiped at the tears on her face. 'After we're out of this mess.'

As Luc's daughter continued to comfort him and Sarah continued to berate Rudy, I looked around for Eric.

I wouldn't have wanted Eric to get between Rudy and Luc, but I'd never seen my son shrink from a fight.

So where was he now? Could he have gone after Verdeaux to stop her? Or make sure she didn't get hurt? I grabbed a lantern and went to slip out the door. Frank came running.

'I'm going to find Eric,' I told the sheepdog. 'You'll be fine here.'

As I said, Frank was a sheepdog of few words. He simply turned tail and looked at the assemblage.

Tien was attending to Luc.

Luc was drunkenly protesting that he was fine.

Sarah was still giving Rudy hell.

Rudy, wisely, was accepting it.

Jacque was watching them appreciatively.

Caron was sipping, equally appreciatively, from a white paper cone.

Bernie, having found himself supplanted by a brandy a fraction of his age, was asleep on the couch.

Oliver was sitting alone, back against the wall.

Mrs G reclined in the shampoo chair, fast asleep with her head hanging over the wash basin.

'Point taken,' I said to Frank. 'If anyone moves, bite them.'

And I slipped out into the hallway.

TWENTY-THREE

To the left of me was An's, where, presumably, Naomi Verdeaux had gone to retrieve her coat from Aurora's body in the freezer.

Brrr. The idea was chilling in more ways than one.

And why did Eric decide to do a walk-about? Granted, he was a curious kid – no, *man*, now – but I didn't see my son trailing after Naomi Verdeaux, a woman he'd just met, especially when, however siren-like, she wouldn't be attractive to him. Yet another thing to be grateful for.

On the other hand, surveying the damage to the old wing might appeal to him. As far as the light of my little lantern reached, the hallway ceiling to my left seemed largely intact, despite the feeling of impending doom I'd experienced as I pounded on the barbershop door. Seven ceiling tiles down, but that was about the extent of the damage.

Still, who knew what lingered beyond the light?

To my right was Uncommon Grounds, in the new part of the mall and, as far as I knew, with no storm-related problems at all.

What it did have, though, was Eric's favorite energy drink.

I turned right.

So nice to have suspects accusing each other, I thought as I made my way down the hall. Eliminates an awful lot of pesky thinking.

Not that thinking had gotten me closer to the truth, anyway. My name badge chart was now buried, and almost certainly water-smeared. But even if the Hannah Montana pen contained waterproof ink and the name badges were laminated, I'm not sure how much good it would have done me. Information is one thing, but knowing how it fits together is something entirely different.

Arriving at Uncommon Grounds' door, I turned the knob and got a sinking feeling. It was locked. Had I locked the door when Frank and I left? I didn't think so.

The answer, of course, was that Caron had returned to lock it. She was the responsible one, after all. The business partner who had affairs, dyed her hair red and then blonde, was having a boob hoist, had gotten dead drunk on brandy old-fashioneds, made out with her husband on a lawn chair and a couch, and was now trying to stave off a hangover with more of the poison that had produced it.

She was the responsible one.

Boy, was Uncommon Grounds in trouble.

Not to mention yours truly, who, as of today had managed to lose her son in a shopping mall twice.

The first was when Eric was six years old and decided it would be fun to disappear into the center of a circular dress rack and stand on the base so his little feet wouldn't show. It was hide-and-go-seek, he said. Eric was hiding, I was the one shrieking hysterically. Damn game should be renamed.

But as frightening as that might have been, this one topped it, what with our being in what might be just the middle stage of a hundred-year storm.

And, oh yeah, with a brutal murderer on the loose.

OK, stop and reason this through. If Caron had locked the door to our shop, Eric would not have been able to get in, either. If he'd even tried.

So where was he?

As I turned away from the door, I heard a click.

'Mom?'

I lifted the lantern. My son had a canned energy drink in his hand.

'Eric.' I grabbed him and gave him a hug. 'I was so worried about you. When I saw that the door was locked, I figured you couldn't be inside.'

'Unless, of course –' he stood aside to let me pass through – 'I was already inside and locked the door like you did at Goddard's and Rudy's. You know,' he smirked, 'to keep us safe.'

Have I expressed sufficiently my dislike of smart-assed teenagers, including my own, on occasion?

I tried a motherly scold. 'You shouldn't have gone anywhere without telling me. You could have been killed.'

How many parents, when they say those words, mean them literally?

Eric's face changed. 'Sorry. I just needed to think and with the wrestling exhibition and all, it was tough.'

There was that.

'Is something wrong?' I asked.

'You mean besides the blizzard, totaling the van and being trapped in a shopping mall with eleven people, two dead bodies, one sheepdog and no running water? All we're missing is a partridge in a pear tree.'

The child has his mother's sense of humor. More's the pity.

'Yes,' I said icily. 'Besides that.'

'You're cold,' Eric said, backing out of the circle of light my lantern was providing. 'Why don't you put on the coat?'

Coat? What coat?

I glanced around.

Everything seemed peaceful, which made me suspicious. Peace in our time not being something one could depend upon.

The litter of our earlier stay was still evident. Cups on the tables. Milk spilled on the counter. I lifted the lantern.

A couple of puddles and a single snowshoe. Bernie's of course. Where were Caron and her paper towels when you needed them?

Probably sleeping it off.

And there, at one table, was Aurora Benson's coat, still draped over a chair. Eric handed it to me.

Pulling it on, I took a second to think about the woman whose coat was giving me warmth.

And whose body would never feel the

garment or any warmth again.

Poor Aurora. I ran my hand over the fur-trimmed collar. I might have made fun of her as the 'Weather Slut', but I had liked her. She would be missed – especially by Oliver. What would he do now?

What would we all do now? Uncommon Grounds was still standing, but more than half the mall was reduced to the kind of rubble I'd always associated with hurricanes and tornados. Would it be rebuilt? Torn down? Where would we go?

Since that wasn't a dilemma we could solve before day-break, it didn't bear thinking about.

I pulled the coat closer around me and counted my blessings. Eric, not only here, but safe and sound as well. Pavlik. God, I wished *he* was here. Him and his buttery leather jacket. They'd know what to do.

A boom of thunder brought me back to cold, dark reality.

'Did you say the van is totaled?'

'Kind of.' Eric pointed to the nearest table. 'Want to sit down? I need to talk to you about something.'

Uh-oh.

I must have looked startled because Eric hastened to reassure me. 'It's nothing to do with me, really. I just need some advice.' He hesitated. 'For a friend.'

Uh-oh, squared. I thought I might need fortification for this.

I eyed the coffee pot sitting on the heating element of the brewer. With no electricity, of course, the coffee would be as cold as the room. Still, it was coffee.

I took a heavy white cup from the rack next to the cash register and poured myself half a cup. Then I opened the small refrigerator under the counter and took out a carton of cream. It was still cool, if not cold. I took a sniff. Smelled OK to me. I dumped a fair amount in the cup, stirred it and took a sip. It needed sweetening. I added Splenda and took a taste.

Damn near perfect. Considering.

Setting the coffee down on a table, I got Eric another energy drink and beckoned him over to me.

I put the lantern down and we settled into the seats across from each other. 'Give.'

Eric played with the pop-top of the drink he held in his hands. 'So I have a friend—'

I interrupted. 'You don't have to use the "friend" thing. Just tell me. It'll be OK.'

He looked affronted. 'But I *do* have a friend.'

'I'm sure you have lots of friends, Sweetie.' I put my hand on his.

'Can it, Mom.'

Ahh, there was the son I knew and loved. Most of the time.

'This isn't about me.' He was getting downright ornery all of a sudden.

'All right.' I waited.

He broke the pop-top right off the can and, irritated, winged it across the store. The aluminum top hit the front window and fell to the floor.

'Eric, you know better than that,' I snapped. 'Pick it up.'

Why this was so important to me I didn't know. The ceiling might come crashing down on us at any moment. One pop-top among the ruins wasn't going to make a whole lot of difference.

'Will not,' Eric snapped back. He stood up. 'I don't even know why I try to talk to you.'

And with that, he stomped out of the shop.

I sat for a second. God, I was bad at this. No wonder Eric had never told me he was gay. I was too busy telling him to pick up his dirty socks.

And yet, there was something reassuring in the exchange.

I'd been being careful with Eric – and Eric,

with me – all day. Just now, though, we'd been ... normal. Eric had told me that he was gay and then we'd moved on. He felt secure enough to be himself. And I'd done the same.

I just wished 'myself' was a better listener.

With a sigh, I got up and took a pen from the coffee mug turned pencil holder next to our cash register. As long as I had the benefit of silence, I might as well try once again to organize my thoughts.

I looked around for paper. Nothing out here in the store, but there would be plenty in the office.

Unfortunately, Caron *had* locked that door.

So what would I write on? A napkin was more appropriate for passing phone numbers in bars than for memorizing deductive reasoning.

I opened the cabinet door. Inside, the checklist of duties I'd written up when our store opened. A scot over a year before.

A year. And what would happen to us now? Starting over someplace new didn't bear thinking about. Besides, Caron and I still hadn't turned enough of a profit to allow us to pay ourselves more than a meager salary. How would we afford to rent – much less maybe outfit – a new space?

Like I said, it didn't bear thinking about just then. So I didn't.

Instead, I took the pen and checklist over to the table and sat down.

I turned over the sheet so I could write on the back, then began to ponder. Ponderously, at that.

To the best of my recollection, I'd figured that anyone but Caron, Sarah and me could have killed Way. It was a little more difficult to know where everyone was when Aurora died, since it was tougher to keep track of people in the pharmacy than it had been in Uncommon Grounds.

I wrote down the names of my suspects, most of whom were also neighbors and friends. The life of a detective is a lonely one.

I topped the list with my favorite nominee for the title of murderer: Naomi Verdeaux, who was neither neighbor nor friend. Now that I had an idea of who had opportunity, it was time to think about motive again.

And motive was tough. Yes, Verdeaux could have found out that Way was seeing Aurora again and killed him in anger. And Aurora, too.

Thing was, I didn't think Naomi Verdeaux really cared for anyone except herself. She bedded men in order to get things from them. Essentially, she shtupps to conquer.

But ... killing the two people who could give her what she wanted, leaving only the one family member who wouldn't – Oliver? It was stupid.

Unless she *was* planning to shtupp Oliver, too. Her idea of an eighteenth birthday present for him.

No, Verdeaux might have the nerve to kill, but she would never desecrate her precious coat by killing Aurora when the other woman was wearing it. Then again, maybe she wanted the coat back because it contained evidence that could implicate her.

I restrained a high-pitched squeal of despair. Why was this so tough? *Some*one hated these people enough to kill them. But who?

The problem was that I couldn't imagine taking another human's life except to protect Eric. And probably myself. OK, definitely myself.

But read the newspaper articles, watch CNN's television reports, and you know that people kill each other for lots of reasons. Suddenly an idea for categorizing the reasons as motives struck me.

The Seven Deadly Sins: Pride, Lust, Gluttony, Greed, Sloth, Wrath and...

Oh, yeah. Envy. Like when I drove past my ex's big house. To my credit, though, I have not killed him. Mostly, these days, I feel sorry for him.

If Verdeaux had murdered Way and Aurora, I didn't think it would be because of greed. She had better avenues available to her to achieve what she wanted by way of material goods. No, for her it would have to be pride. I wrote that sin down next to Verdeaux's name.

Pleased with myself, I moved on to the next name on my list. Jacque Oui.

Naomi Verdeaux's new store could well put Jacque's off-site market out of business. But then he should have killed his ex-wife, not Way and Aurora.

Verdeaux might have a point, though. Maybe Aurora, wearing Verdeaux's coat, had been mistaken for her. Jacque killing both his ex-wife and Way out of anger, I might be able to understand. And it would be 'wrath'.

I liked this seven sins thing. Gave me a framework for my guesswork.

Then there was Oliver. His father ignored him, but according to Verdeaux, Way was taking care of Oliver's future. Of course, making your son a lifetime janitor at a strip mall paled in comparison to your dying –

along with your ex-wife – thus leaving the mall to your son.

So that meant Oliver's motive would be greed. And maybe a touch of wrath and pride for good measure. Not to mention loyalty (not exactly a sin, granted) to Mrs G, who would be not only storeless but, without Goddard's Pharmacy, homeless in the bargain.

I really couldn't see Mrs G killing Way or Aurora, though if she had, it probably would have been pride, maybe combined with wrath. Pride, in fearing she was going to be out on the street, and wrath, in hating how the couple treated her surrogate grandson.

Rudy was next on the list. He was the one tenant who didn't mind leaving the mall. In fact, he apparently was in bed, figuratively and literally, with Verdeaux. Had he killed Aurora, thinking she was Verdeaux? But if so, why kill Way first? I thought for a second and put down 'envy', with a little 'lust' thrown in.

Tien. Nah, I couldn't see it. Then again, if she did have a crush on Way ... I thought for another few seconds and put down 'lust', only in tiny letters.

Her father Luc was a more likely suspect. If Tien was threatened in some way, I thought her father would be capable – both physically and attitudinally – of killing to protect her. And, under those circumstances, I could see Tien lying to give her father an alibi.

But why would Way and Aurora be a threat to Tien or to Luc? The closing of An's was a shame and obviously a real blow to both of them. Still, Luc seemed to be looking at it philosophically, saying it was a chance for Tien to move on to a life of her own. And maybe one of his as well.

Question was, did Luc mean it? I shrugged my shoulders and wrote down 'pride'. I'd read somewhere that pride was the emotion that all the other sins stemmed from, so it became my fallback position.

Last on the list was Bernie. Nah, again. Theoretically, I supposed it was possible that he'd snowshoed in earlier, killed Way and then waited around for hours to kill Aurora, backtrack to find Eric in the ditch and arrive at Benson Plaza.

And if all that weren't improbable enough, the only possible motive would be that he thought Caron and Way were having an affair. Given that Bernie hadn't killed the other man Caron had ... seen, I didn't give that theory much weight. Besides, Bernie genuinely loved the trollop and he'd have no motive for killing Aurora.

And then, out of sight and out of mind, was the 'mystery man' who bowled me over when Frank went into defense mode.

I sat back. When you came down to it, some people had a reason for wanting to be rid of Way. And some, Aurora. But...

I stopped.

Way had been meat-cleavered to death and then snow-blowed. I couldn't be sure how Aurora had been killed, but whatever it was, it had to have penetrated the hood of the coat she was wearing.

Luc and Tien had meat cleavers, Oliver a snow-blower. Rudy displayed all kinds of blades, Mrs G had her husband's guns. Was this some vengeful re-enactment of *Murder on the Orient Express*? Had everybody lent a helping hand?

Which was when my brave little lantern flickered its last and went out.

TWENTY-FOUR

I sat stock still. The snow outside created some light, but it didn't penetrate far into the store. I felt for the lantern and, finding it, turned the switch off and then on again. Nothing. Apparently AA batteries don't regenerate.

Standing up, I closed my eyes, counted to ten and reopened them. Pupils properly dilated now, I could at least make out shapes. It wasn't as good as even the dim emergency lights fueled by the generator, of course, but I was able to see my way to the door.

Pulling it open and stepping into the hallway, matters didn't improve much at all, light-wise. In fact, the hall was in total darkness. Still, I should be able to feel my way down past The Bible Store to Rudy's.

I figured touching and tapping my fingers along the wall would be easy and it was. Until the wall disappeared, and I fell into a void. The electrical closet. It was where the circuit breakers for the mall were located, along with the connection to the nonfunctional generator which had to be outside. But did it have to be nonfunctional?

After Way started the generator, Rudy had come looking for gas to keep it going. Had he found it or did the discovery of Way's body divert...

I was picturing Way's body with the meat cleaver in it. The meat cleaver I had originally thought was the handle of a short shovel, just as Oliver and Caron had.

And, in that instant, I knew who had killed Way and Aurora.

A moment later, I also realized another person was in danger.

Standing there in the dark, though, what was I going to be able to do about it?

I searched in my pocket and found the second of my 'Two for $4.99' Stir Wars swizzle sticks. By the neon green glow I found my way out of the electrical closet and into the narrow – if not straight – service corridor.

I crossed to the other side of the hall to avoid the small storage rooms and janitor's closets. Despite my stir-stick, I still had to resume feeling my way along. As I passed

The Bible Store, my hand landed on the knob.

It moved. Only a quarter turn, maybe, but the door had been locked the last time I checked, which was just before I found Way's body. I'd heard noises inside and, assuming someone was hurt, I'd tried to get in. I rubbed my shoulder in remembrance of my one and, believe me, *only* attempt to break down a door.

Mindful of Luc's earlier example, I first turned the knob and then pulled the door. It opened.

When I'd found Frank pounding his furry head against the storeroom door of Uncommon Grounds, I figured the noise that I'd earlier thought was coming from The Bible Store next door was, indeed, Frank.

Now I wasn't so sure.

I cautiously held the little stir-stick out in front of me, for all the good it did. Memo to file: a swizzle stick's radius of ambient light is about five inches.

I moved into the room and immediately tripped over something big on the floor.

I said a word I don't say in front of Eric, because I'd banged my shin against something. It was a good hurt, though, because it didn't feel like a body.

273

I shined the light down.

A bicycle. What in...?

No, wait ... Two bikes.

I stepped over the bikes and cautiously looked around. As in Uncommon Grounds, the reflection of the snow through the store windows improved visibility a bit.

Using the white glow from outside, I moved to the antique oak table that held the cash register.

And, sure enough, the money drawer was open and empty.

Now, this didn't necessarily scream robbery to me. Caron and I routinely left our register with its empty drawer out. That way, anyone scoping out the place could see, even from beyond the windows, that there was no money still in the shop. Why burgle a business that had already deposited its daily harvest at the bank?

The Bible Store's register, though, still had a few coins in it. And there was a ring of keys – evidently tossed carelessly – on the table. They'd been wet, because the beautifully restored wood underneath them showed the only milky watermark on its surface.

I didn't want to touch the keys, so I used my swizzle stick to shift them for a better look at the fob.

Hyundai. And next to the car tag on the ring was a tiny charm. A red hat tied with a purple ribbon.

These were Sophie's keys. Sophie Daystrom, Red Hat Lady and owner of the Hyundai that had been vandalized this morning, apparently by two guys on bikes.

Rubbing my shin, I figured I'd found their mode of transportation.

Given all that had happened at Benson Plaza since my talk with Sophie, I had to reach back for the details of our conversation. She'd said the thieves had taken her keys. It looked now as though they'd used them to get in and rob the place. They'd also stashed their bikes, maybe because they figured the two-wheelers might be traced to them. Or, alternatively, because the robbers, like Pavlik and his Harley, couldn't ride through the deepening snow.

Now that I was looking for the right telltale signs I could see that the store's drawers had been hastily opened and closed, just as the ones in Way's office. I had no way of knowing what might have been taken here either, but Sophie ought to be able to help the police on that.

Next, I turned my attention to the shelves lined with holy books of different types.

275

They looked untouched except for one that had been knocked to the floor. There was a gap on one shelf big enough to have held another volume equal in thickness to the one at my feet.

The thieves had taken a Bible?

Chewing on that, I carefully stepped over the bicycles and let myself out of the store, leaving everything as I'd found it, except for the tickled keys.

Trusty stir-stick in hand, I made my way to the barbershop door, where presumably all survivors and one murderer were passing their snowbound time.

Then I kept going.

TWENTY-FIVE

Light by swizzle stick is not perfect, but it did get me to the door of An's Foods without mishap, despite the debris in the service corridor.

I wasn't sure what I'd find inside, so I hesitated before knocking. Then, taking a deep breath and rapping my knuckles on the door, I called out.

'Naomi?'

A beat. 'Are you in there?'

Two beats. 'Is there damage?'

Verdeaux didn't answer. Neither did the damage.

Cracking open the door, I sidewinded across the threshold. I couldn't see much by the light I held, but the flashes of lightning reflecting off the clouds and snow again penetrated enough to show me that the whole side of the store, the one closest to Goddard's, had, indeed, collapsed. As I looked further, another ceiling tile fell to the floor shattering maybe a yard from where I was standing.

What in the hell was I doing there?

'Naomi?' Same effort, same result.

I hadn't heard the woman referred to by her first name by anyone, except Caron when she was half in the bag. I wasn't too sure I had standing to take notice, though, since I still called my boy-toy (or so I liked to imagine, though 'fantasize' was probably more accurate) Pavlik, instead of Jake.

'Ms Verdeaux?' Formality, but still nothing. I didn't think trying 'Hey, Predatory Manipulative Slut' would garner a response either.

The big locker/freezer where we had consigned Way and Aurora was on the back wall of the store, behind the meat counter and deli. Both the locker and the counter appeared to be intact, but I approached cautiously, keeping an eye out for falling objects. Oh, and murderers. Not to mention Bible-stealing, bicycle-riding bandits.

I hadn't stopped at the barbershop, because I couldn't chance alerting the killer. In retrospect, that might have been short-sighted.

Safely to the deli section, I slipped behind the counter. The freezer door was closed tight, so if Verdeaux was still in the market she was huffing pretty frosty air.

If she was trapped in the meat locker, the coat on Aurora's body – assuming Verdeaux had been able to pry it off her – might keep Ms Gross-National alive, though I had no idea for how long. Other than that, I couldn't imagine why any normal woman, cold or not, would want clothing in which another woman had been murdered.

As I pulled on the locker handle, my stir-stick barely illuminated some of the work area behind the meat case. A number of deli and butcher tools had been laid out, presumably to be packed or sold. Next to them were canned goods, stacked in neat rows.

Swinging open the freezer's door and bracing it with my heel, I stood outside the threshold, waiting for a blast of air to pass, measurably colder than that in the store or the service corridor.

Then, holding the light ahead of me, I peered into the freezer. Or tried to. The swizzle stick flashlight worked about as well as it did inside the service hallway. Which was not much.

'Dammit,' I said out loud. 'I feel like I'm in an episode of the X-Files.'

I moved my meager light source around. My eyes were slowly adjusting to the near pitch-dark. Close to me I could make out bags of what looked like frozen vegetables, tubs of something, and ... Yup, I could confirm Way was still on the shelf and Aurora, still in the cart.

But, what was that over by the corner?

Shit, shit, shit. It could be nothing, or it could be Naomi Verdeaux crumpled into a heap. I had no way of knowing, unless I moved into the locker. And I'd seen too many movies where the stupid heroine enters a room – or a meat freezer or a tanning bed –and ends up trapped. And dead.

'Stupidcide' I think they call it.

I considered the situation. If I went over the threshold, I could become the heap in the other corner. And I certainly never had an empathetic moment in the presence of Naomi Verdeaux.

Still ... she was another human being.

I looked around for something I could put in the jamb to keep the heavy door from closing behind me. Let's see: scale, meat slicer, cleaver...

I settled on a can of kidney beans.

Using the container as a doorstop, I stepped into the freezer. Cautiously approaching the corner, I shone my light on the dark pile.

I had been holding my breath, I realized, and now I let it out. Then I wasn't sure if I should have.

The heap was not Naomi Verdeaux.

It was, however, her coat.

The question, of course, was why would Verdeaux have come in here and wrestled the coat off a frozen body, only to leave the fur on the floor. Had she been interrupted?

Even as I had the thought, I heard a noise behind me.

Grabbing the coat, I ran to the door.

Sure enough, it was closed tight. Either my kidney beans had let me down or someone had intervened, shutting me inside the freezer with two corpses, frozen peas and a couple of tubs of margarita mix.

At least I wouldn't die of starvation. Cold, yes, (subtract another five degrees for my anxiety level), but not starvation. Or even scurvy.

And why in the hell hadn't we had margaritas instead of those lousy old-fashioneds?

I realized I was still holding Verdeaux's coat, petting it like a dog with my rapidly numbing fingers. Next thing I'd be talking to it, like Tom Hanks did in that movie where he was marooned on a tropical island. Except this wasn't a volley ball.

OK, OK, Maggy. Settle down. No need to get hysterical here. Think.

I concentrated on the coat, slowing my breathing. Someone would come looking for me. Eventually.

I petted the coat again. At least, I think I did. My fingers were no longer transmitting micro-climate news to my brain.

I might never see Eric again. Or Frank. Or Pavlik. Or Pavlik's jacket.

A little sob escaped me.

As I took my hand from the coat, I touched something crusty. Aurora's blood, of course. I couldn't tell if the crustiness was because it had dried or frozen or both.

But I felt something else, too, and now I moved the stir stick closer to examine it.

A bullet hole.

I didn't have experience with guns, not the way I did with less noisy methods of dealing death. On the other hand, I probably watch-ed as much television as anyone else.

The hole had been hidden in the fur of the hood, but now that the caked blood had matted everything down, it was obvious.

So, Aurora had been shot.

And I was still stuck in a freezer.

I pounded on the door, my closed fist without any feeling in it at all. 'Is anybody out there?'

Preferably someone without a gun?

I heard a crash through the door. Whether it was thunder or a gunshot, I couldn't tell.

Dropping the coat, I redoubled my efforts. Meaning I pounded on the door with two numbed fists. That's when I brushed against something round and flat on the door. A door knob?

I tried to turn the thing and pull. It turned all right, but that didn't seem to produce any results. So, I tried to slide it up, then slide it down. Still nothing.

So I used my marginally less-frozen fist to just pound the knob itself.

Thanks be to God if the door didn't swing open.

I rubbed my less-frozen fist, with my more frozen one. I didn't know which hurt more. The one I'd just smacked the door with would be bruised tomorrow to match my shoulder and my shin, but I was free.

I should have known there would be an emergency release. This was the twenty-first century, where we're protected from everything but our own ignorance.

I stepped out of the freezer and into the market proper. Truth be told, the store was nearly as cold as the freezer. Maybe we would have been better off leaving Way and Aurora outside the freezer, even outside the mall, as we'd found them.

I heard another crack. A more distinct version of what came through the freezer door.

I looked up.

The ceiling tiles above me were gone and through the framework I could see the flat roof of the shopping mall. As I watched, there was another crack, louder and longer than the others. As I turned to run, there was a really loud crash and the butt end of a joist hit the ground between me and the hallway door.

As debris and snow rained down, I made for the front door instead. It was locked, but you can't say I hadn't learned from my mistakes. I turned the deadbolt and pushed the door as hard as I could.

With a strength borne of desperation and downright terror, I managed to push the door hard enough to clear the snow now piled in front of it. I squeezed through the small opening and waded into the thigh-deep snow on the sidewalk, trying to get away from the building. When I hit the curb buried in the snow, I fell forward into the parking lot.

As I landed face-down in the snow, I heard a familiar sound.

'Pfft.'

Because the temperature was hovering just below freezing, the bottom couple inches of what had been snow was now slush. I raised my face out of the muck and looked around.

The snowfall was finally letting up and the clouds had thinned a bit. The slightest of glows in the east signaled that dawn was approaching, if not imminent. It was enough, though, to backlight the landscape.

A winter wonderland of sorts. Snow clung to everything. Telephone wires, street signs, tree branches that already had begun to bud. Under one of the maples at the corner of the building, Rudy and Naomi Verdeaux were in a clinch. Verdeaux didn't have a coat on, but I didn't think Rudy was trying to keep her warm.

I pushed myself up, the slush falling off Aurora's coat in sloshing globs. As I stood, Rudy, whose back was toward me, turned.

'It's over, Rudy,' I said. 'Why don't you just let her go?'

'I can't,' he said. 'I love her.'

Apparently 'her' didn't feel the same way. Wrapped in Rudy's arms, Verdeaux said nothing.

'I understand.' I moved closer. 'Naomi made you feel young. You had her, even if you weren't town chairman anymore. It made you feel important, having a beautiful woman on your arm. Then you realized she didn't care about any relationship with you.'

Rudy just looked at me. I was near enough now to see tears in his eyes.

'I felt the same way when Ted left me,' I continued, 'and I left my job. Eric was off at school to boot, and I wasn't sure who I was anymore. If I'm not Maggy Thorsen of First National, or Ted's wife, or Eric's mother, who was I?'

'You are still Eric's mother,' Rudy muttered. 'I have no one.'

'You're right.' I was continuing to move – slowly – toward them. 'Even if Eric is away, I *am* still his mother. But you're still someone, too.'

Rudy laughed.

I wasn't quite seeing the humor in it. I pointed at the lightening sky. 'It's nearly morning and the snow has let up. We can get out of here soon.'

He laughed a little harder.

I paused a beat. Two. 'You can get out of here. Just let Naomi go, Rudy.'

A 'pfft' from Verdeaux and Rudy shrugged,

dropping his arms to his outer thighs.

Naomi sank into the snow, a pair of gardening shears now visible even in the poor light. The shears were sticking out prominently from between her shoulder blades.

And I, Maggy Thorsen, mother of Eric, promised myself and my son that I wouldn't join her.

At least, not that day.

TWENTY-SIX

'Imaginative,' I said, backing away. Naomi Verdeaux lay in the snow, her head turned sideways, her eyes staring and already starting to cloud over. I'd been too late at every stage. I wondered how long he'd stood there, holding her.

'First, Luc's meat cleaver,' I said, backing up farther, 'then a bullet from ... whose gun?'

'Hank Goddard's hunting rifle.' Rudy was staring down at Naomi's body. When he looked up at me, his eyes were blank. 'It was in the bathroom. Gloria was careless to leave it there. Somebody could have gotten hurt.'

Fine time to worry. 'But why Aurora, Rudy? And why Way in the first place?'

'He took it from me.'

'Took what?' I was biding my time, hoping for sunrise. I didn't know what I expected. Pavlik on a garbage truck, plowing to my rescue?

'Everything!' Suddenly Rudy's voice rumbled like a thunderclap from the storm in the cold, dark lot. His eyes weren't blank anymore, and he raised his fist to the sky. 'I counted. I was important. First, Way Benson took my town chairmanship. Then he took her.'

Rudy glanced down at his latest victim. Crumpled as Verdeaux was, she could almost be kneeling. Kneeling at his feet. Rudy would like that.

'Then they took my shop, the two of them.' He spat on Verdeaux's body.

I started forward before reminding myself that Naomi was beyond feeling the insult. And it could get me killed.

Rudy looked up and something in his eyes ignited. It looked like 'wrath'. Dante called it 'love of justice perverted to revenge'.

Perverted was right.

Rudy kept ranting. 'Way told me what they'd done, you know, when I saw him outside. That Naomi had set out to get me to sign over my lease. And, with her ... charms, she succeeded.'

Rudy looked like he was going to spit again.

'But maybe Way was lying,' I tried. By now I'd managed to retreat one small, slow step at a time, to the barbershop's front window. 'Naomi loved you. Truly.' Hogwash, but I figured it was worth a try.

Or not.

Rudy laughed in the same humorless way he had just before he dropped Naomi's body. 'What do you think I am, an idiot?'

'No. No, of course not.' A homicidal maniac, maybe, but not an idiot.

'But again, Rudy: why Aurora?'

A shrug. 'My only slip-up. She passed by my barbershop window when I was looking for the brandy and I mistook her for Naomi because of Aurora being all bundled up in Naomi's coat.' Another shrug. 'Mistakes do happen, you know.'

Smiling – grimly, but smiling – I tried to see into his shop window.

'Don't bother. They're gone.'

'Gone?' Terror pooled in the pit of my stomach. Eric? Could Rudy possibly have...

He gestured toward what was left of Benson Plaza. 'I told them the roof, over even my place, was going down and I sent them to Uncommon Grounds. Told them to wait there while I went to find you and Naomi.'

Another glance at her body. 'I found her.' A grin directed toward me. 'And now, you've found me.'

I didn't like the logic he saw in closing the circle.

I slid along the front of the store under the eaves to the corner, then turned and ran toward Uncommon Grounds.

In truth, it was more slogging than running, so I chanced a glance over my shoulder. Rudy had already rounded the corner, but he had to contend with the snow, too, and I was younger than he was. I would make it to Uncommon Grounds and even if the door was locked, I could...

I slammed smack-dab into Pavlik's Harley parked on the sidewalk, tipping it over and landing me face down in the snow.

Again.

It seemed like a lifetime ago, when I'd run out of An's and fell before I saw Rudy with Naomi. If I'd reacted faster, if I hadn't stupidly gotten myself stuck in the freezer, could I have been there in time to save her life?

I didn't know, but I was damned if I was going to let Rudy get away with the lives of three people. Four, counting me. And then what? Would he kill everyone in the mall like one of those psycho misfits who storm schools and malls, clutching a gun and wanting to be someone?

Would he kill Eric? And Frank?

I lifted my face out of the slush and, in a moment of déjà vu, saw Rudy again. This time, though, he was silhouetted by the sun just starting to peek up over the horizon.

Dawn. And no snowplow. Worse, no Pavlik.

Worst of all, Rudy was still coming, maybe the ability to wade through those flooded rice paddies holding him in good stead now in the deep snow.

I screamed and tried to scramble to my feet, but one leg, from knee to foot, was pinned beneath the motorcycle. Turning on my side, I tried to get leverage to squirm out from under the Harley.

As I did, Rudy leapt over the bike. Damned if all that work at the gym hadn't paid off. His physical prowess wasn't what worried me, though. Rudy had a straight razor in his hand. Open, like a jackknife.

Shades of *Sweeney Todd*.

Starring Johnny Depp. Rent that one, too.

I put my arm up to protect my throat and face against Rudy's first slash. His blade caught in Aurora's thick coat. Swearing, he grabbed my arm and tried to pull it away from my face. I resisted, rolling face down.

As I did, a final clap of thunder sounded overhead.

And then silence.

Cautiously taking my arm down, I saw Mrs G, handbag in her left hand and the revolver from the cash register in her right.

TWENTY-SEVEN

Eric and Oliver came forward to lift the motorcycle while Jacque helped me slide my leg out from under.

Luc took the gun Mrs G offered him. I probably should have felt better with the revolver in experienced hands. On the other hand, the widow of a deer hunter had done herself – and him – proud.

'You saved my life, you know,' I told Mrs G. 'And maybe everybody else's.'

She waved me off. 'Hank was the one with the hunting permit. If I fired a gun a dozen times in my life, that was a lot. He must have guided my hand.'

If Hank was aiming from heaven, he must have been one hell of a sharpshooter. The bullet struck Rudy in the shoulder, the impact knocking him sideways and away from me.

Rudy was groaning as Mrs G moved away, and I had an urge to kick snow in his face.

He'd killed three people because his ego had been bruised and now *he* was whining?

Though whining and screaming admittedly had their place. Apparently my screaming had brought a posse: one sheepdog, seven survivors armed with Uncommon Grounds coffee cups and butter knives, and one old lady toting a lethal weapon.

'Are you OK, Mom?' Eric asked me anxiously.

I threw my arms around him. 'I am *so* sorry I yelled at you because of the pop-top.'

'Honestly? I kind of liked it.' He pulled back so he could look at me.

'You know, I kind of liked it, too,' I admitted. 'It was...'

'Normal,' Eric finished for me.

And normal was good. Normal was better than good.

I saw Oliver standing nearby, listening. He looked away, embarrassed.

I beckoned him over. 'Your Mom and Dad did love you, you know.'

Oliver tried to say something, but the words turned into a sob.

Eric and I, with one arm around the other, reached out to pull Oliver into a three-way clinch.

'Group hug,' Eric called, and I felt Oliver's

body relax at Eric's light tone.

The younger boy's forehead was pressed against my shoulder. He sniffled once and took a deep breath. 'Did Eric tell you?'

Now Eric tensed up.

Go with the flow. 'He tried to. But I didn't give him the chance.'

Oliver nodded and cleared his throat. 'I ... umm, I did something bad.'

'Let me guess. You and a friend on bikes broke into a bunch of cars. You stole Sophie Daystrom's keys and the two of you let yourselves into The Bible Store.' I figured that pretty much covered it.

Oliver tried to back out of the clinch, but I didn't let him.

Eric knew me well enough to just keep quiet.

'A *Bible* Store, Oliver?' I was trying to understand.

'Petey said we would just look around, but—'

Wait a second.

'Petey? The kid who shovels my snow?' Or didn't, most of the time. This was the 'mystery man' who knocked me down? Wait until I got hold of him.

'Yeah, I—'

'You stay away from Petey,' I hissed. 'Do

you hear me?'

'Yes, ma'am, I ummm...'

On a roll, I turned to Eric. 'And you. No littering.'

He wisely took a page out of Oliver's book. 'Yes, ma'am.'

'And ... stay safe, do you hear me?' Even I heard the crack in my voice.

Eric squeezed me hard. 'I will. Don't worry.'

'And you, Oliver,' I said, turning back to him. 'Petey is no good. And he's a lousy shoveler.'

'Yes, ma'am. Uh, if it matters, the cars weren't locked.'

'It doesn't,' I said flatly. 'They are someone else's cars, sitting on someone else's property. Speaking of other people's property, did you go back to The Bible Store and steal a book?'

Oliver didn't answer.

'Oliver.' I knew there was an ominous warning tone in my voice. I'd practiced it on Eric for years.

Oliver squirmed. 'Mrs G. She's been so sad. I thought maybe the Bible stories would make her feel better.'

That didn't excuse it, of course, but he didn't steal something for himself, like...

'You hid it behind the magazines in the book rack, didn't you?' I said, remembering the scene at Goddard's. 'I thought you'd taken a dirty book to the bathroom.'

'Uh-uh,' Oliver said. 'It was later when I took the dirty magazine.'

Eric laughed. I squeezed his head.

'Did you steal anything else from The Bible Store, Oliver?'

'Nah. I think Petey would have, but there was just coins in the cash register. Sales must not be good.'

Small wonder. It was like setting up a salt lick in Sodom and Gomorrah.

'What about your dad's office? One of the drawers was forced. What did you take from there?'

'My dad's office? Nothing, we ... ohhhh...'

'What?' I squeezed Oliver's head this time.

'I just went in there to see if I could find out what was happening with the mall. The drawer was already broken, which is why my dad only kept the phone book in it. And I didn't break in, honestly. I had a key.'

I didn't point out that they'd also had a key for The Bible Store. It just had been a stolen key.

A tap on my shoulder.

'The cavalry's coming,' Sarah's voice said.

298

We broke the huddle. As I turned, I heard a rumble.

A snowplow, cutting a swath. Behind the plow was a fire truck and, behind that, a county sheriff's squad car.

'Poor Aurora,' I said to Jake Pavlik that afternoon.

Finally, we were sitting on the floor, our backs against the couch in front of my over-sized fireplace. My economy-sized sheepdog was lying next to me. My gay son had gone out to help clear sidewalks and driveways for people who couldn't do it themselves.

'Wrong place, wrong time,' Pavlik said nodding.

'Plus, wrong coat,' I said. Aurora's murder had been a case of mistaken identity, just as Naomi Verdeaux had thought. 'Naomi suspected Oliver, not Rudy.'

'Which probably cost Verdeaux her life. Rudy confessed to everything, by the way,' Pavlik said. 'I never liked the guy, but I sure didn't put him down as a killer.'

'His sin was pride,' I said. 'It goeth before a fall.'

Pavlik ran his finger along my jaw line. 'Well, *I'm* proud of *you*. You realized that Rudy was the murderer when you saw him with Verdeaux?'

'Before that,' I said, feeling a little smug and nicely snug. I had Pavlik to the right of me and his jacket to the left. 'I tumbled to it when I thought about the generator.'

'The generator?' Pavlik looked puzzled.

'And the big meat cleaver, which Caron and I both mistook for a shovel handle.'

'Soooo...?' Pavlik knew I was being cryptic on purpose. He hated cryptic.

I, on the other hand, sort of liked the idea of Pavlik hanging on my every word.

Hanging on *me* was even better. I snuggled in deeper, resting my head on his chest. 'So Caron told me she thought there was a snow shovel outside the back door. She wanted me to clear the walks.'

Pavlik grinned. 'Lost cause, I assume?'

'Definitely.' I sat up and turned toward him. 'In fact, it was so distasteful that I put it out of my mind.'

'Until...' Pavlik's patience was wearing thin. Getting dog-eared, even.

I patted Frank. '*Until* I realized that if Caron saw the "shovel", Way had to already be dead.'

Pavlik just gave me the eye this time and waited.

'Don't you see? Rudy came into Uncommon Grounds *after* the electricity went out, *after* Caron saw "the shovel". He said that Way had started the generator.'

Pavlik nodded slowly. 'Which he couldn't have.'

I nodded eagerly. 'Since he had a meat cleaver/shovel sticking out of him. It was Rudy who started the generator after he killed Way. He claimed Way did it to make us think he was still alive.'

'And gave himself an alibi at the same time,' Pavlik said thoughtfully. 'Good thinking.'

'Me? Or Rudy?'

Pavlik was no fool. 'You, of course.'

He smiled, his blue eyes lighting up. Then they darkened. 'I'm afraid the strip mall is in bad shape,' Pavlik said softly. 'You'll likely have to move.'

'I know.' A few seconds of silence.

'That's OK, though,' I said finally.

Frank put his big furry head against me and pushed, his sign he had to go out.

I got up. 'We'll all be OK. Maybe Mrs G and Oliver and Tien and Luc and I can start our own strip mall.'

'Thinking of becoming a real-estate magnate now?' Pavlik asked as I followed Frank to the door.

'Sarah wants in, too,' I said over my shoulder as I escorted the sheepdog out. 'We'll see, though. I think Oliver is going to be OK. He's going to live with Mrs G.'

'That's good,' Pavlik said. 'He's not a bad kid.'

'Nope. He's just ... a kid.' I glanced back at Pavlik, still sitting by the fire. I guess I wanted him to tell me he knew what Oliver had been up to and that he understood why I was keeping it to myself.

I knew it wasn't going to happen. If Pavlik was aware that Oliver had broken the law, he would be honor-bound to do something about it. Anything else would be ... unPavlik. And probably grounds for some sort of horrible legal action.

I wasn't about to put Pavlik in that position. But I also couldn't bear to turn in Oliver, who was an orphan in fact long before he became an orphan in name.

Oliver deserved a second chance. And if lying to Pavlik, who I hoped was the love of my life, was the price I had to pay to give Oliver that second chance in his, I was willing to pay it.

But, believe me, Oliver was going to pay a price, too.

I'd told Mrs G everything. She'd already

302

given Luc the gun, which freed her up to grab Oliver by the ear.

Wincing he'd said, 'This is what you and Eric meant by normal, right?'

'Tough love,' I admitted. 'If she rips it off, though, let me know.'

Mrs G laughed. Then she cried. Then Oliver cried.

They were going to be OK.

As I watched Frank sniff around the yard, I felt myself relax. The sun was shining and the snow was sliding off the roof in mini-avalanches. The drip-drip-drip of the melting snow on the bushes was the only sound.

Suddenly, a 'whoosh'. A snowplow passing, pushing the snow and slush off the road and into my driveway. I hadn't cleared it, since I figured the snow would be melted by tomorrow.

And if Petey came by...

I couldn't let the delinquent escalate his bad behavior. On the other hand, ratting him out would mean blowing the whistle on Oliver, as well.

I planned to sit down with Petey's parents and tell them what he'd done, including knocking me down. Maybe that would work and maybe it wouldn't. In Brookhills, corporal punishment meant taking the car keys away for a week.

Either way, I intended to keep track of Petey. And I was going to inform him I'd be watching. If he made one wrong step, I'd go to the police and tell them everything.

Having made his inspection round, Frank settled on the new sugar maple I'd planted in the middle of the back yard. As he lifted his leg, a plotch of snow from the branches landed splat on his head.

The young tree had taken a beating from the heavy snow, but already it was springing back.

Bent but not broken. The young are like that.